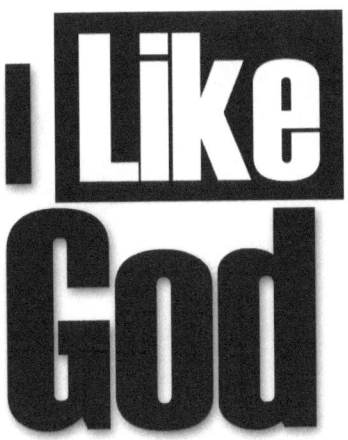

OTHER BOOKS BY JEFF YAGER

Atom and Eve

I Like God

A Novel

Jeff Yager and Skye Bynes

HANNACROIX CREEK BOOKS, INC.
Stamford, Connecticut

Published by:

HANNACROIX CREEK BOOKS, INC.
1127 High Ridge Road, #110
Stamford, Connecticut 06905 USA
hannacroix@aol.com
www.hannacroixcreekbooks.com
Follow us on twitter:
www.twitter.com/hannacroixcreek

ISBN: 978-1-938998-16-4 (hardcover)
978-1-938998-15-7 (trade paperback)
978-1-938998-17-1 (e-book)

LIBRARY OF CONGRESS CATALOGING-IN-PUBLICATION DATA

Yager, Jeff, author.
  I like God
: a novel / Jeff Yager, Skye Bynes.
    pages cm
  ISBN 978-1-938998-16-4
(hardcover) -- ISBN 978-1-938998-15-7 (trade pbk.)
1. Social media--Fiction.
2. Conduct of life--Fiction. I. Bynes, Skye, author. II. Title.

PS3625.A364I3 2015
  813'.6--dc23

      2015022345

Chapter One
The Book of Joey

JOEY TOOK ONE LAST SATISFACTORY BITE, then threw the crumbled up wrapper of his favorite chocolate and almond bar across the room, just missing the garbage pail next to his bed. *That was so damn good,* he thought. He cracked open a cold can of Mountain Mist soda and began to chug it, while searching the Internet. Joey was looking up the average life span of a giraffe.

His closest friends would most likely consider Joey Taylor, a recently unemployed pizza delivery driver, cynical and pessimistic. He stopped dreaming big at the age of 26. He still lived with his parents in the Camden, New Jersey house where he grew up.

Joey's father was African American. His mother was Irish American. Although he was light skinned, most people considered him black. But he typically corrected them by jokingly saying that he was actually a "zebra."

His phone vibrated on the table before he picked it up. It was his girlfriend, Amber.

With a smile forming, he quickly put the phone to his ear.

"Hey Beautiful," Amber said.

"Hey, aren't I supposed to be the one calling you beautiful?" Joey asked.

"Well you are beautiful, and handsome, and amazing, and I love you!"

"I love you too, Boo."

"I get out of work tonight at five thirty. Would you like me to pick up some sushi on the way home? I'm really in the mood for some sushi!" said Amber.

"That sounds amazing! I can pay for it on my credit card."

"Oh nonsense, you know I can afford it, Babe! Plus, I know you are going through a rough patch right now. I don't mind paying for things until you get your new job."

Ugh, she's always like this, Joey thought.

"Babe, I have a credit card. I'll worry about it later. It makes me feel less manly when *you* pay for dinner.

"I won't take *no* for an answer. You took me out to that

amazing Orange Orange! concert last week, so I owe you one."

Joey rolled his eyes as his girlfriend went on.

"I'll see you when I get off work, Hun. I've got to run! Text me what you want from Hiro's! I love you!"

"I love you, too. Talk to you after work."

Joey tossed his phone into the hamper full of dirty clothes. He continued to waste time on his computer, reading random articles and watching funny videos on ViewTube with the TV on in the background for his basic cable cartoons and cooking shows.

Joey had become what most people would call a bum. Like some of his friends, he had no real ambition to get up and do anything most of the time. His friends would always try to get him to go out with them, but he rarely wanted to leave the house.

Two and a half months ago, Joey was a delivery driver at Mikey's Pizzeria, and a pretty good one. Unfortunately, three times in one day, Joey was late dropping off food due to their policy that the pizza will be delivered in 40 minutes or less. He got fired despite four years of hard and dedicated work, showing up on time and covering for his co-workers whenever they needed him to. His customer service was top-notch, and he always received good tips because people liked his personality.

His boss said that Joey cost him too much money that one day and if he didn't pay for the pizzas out of his own pocket, Joey would be fired. Joey refused to pay, and he was fired on the spot.

Joey hadn't been able to get a job since being fired. He was collecting unemployment, but since half of his wages were in tips, he only received $260 a month, which wasn't nearly enough for him to live comfortably.

Amber was a receptionist at a local start-up app company, AllTalk, that was taking off. Joey and Amber had been in love since they met at community college. They met in their second and final year when they took the same film class. They both liked film, but neither took it too far. Joey had always been interested in movies and television, specifically comedies.

As Joey skipped from site to site, there was a loud pounding on the front door of his parents' house.

What the... Joey thought as he leaped down the staircase and ran to the front door. The pounding got louder. *What the fuck? I'm coming, I'm coming,* Joey thought, as he reached the door. He unlocked and opened the door. His best friend Henry was the annoying knocker. "What the hell, man. What's with all the banging?" Joey asked.

"Took you long enough! What's going on, Bro!?" asked his friend, sticking his hand out for a high five.

Joey slapped Henry's hand.

"Dude, you smell like a dang skunk, you know that?" asked Joey. Henry usually came over to the house reeking of marijuana.

"Ohhh man, I didn't even notice!"

Of course, Joey thought.

"I got air freshener in the car if you want me to spray before the parents smell me." Henry pointed to the red, beat-down sports car he'd had since high school.

"Lay off the reefer, my dude. That stuff will fry your brain!" Joey half-laughed.

"You're hilarious, man. Classic Joey," said Henry.

"Come on in, fuck-boy, and run straight up to my room before my mom notices you're here. I don't need her thinking I'm a crackhead like you," Joey laughed.

"Shut up, man. I never smoke crack. That's not cool," Henry said as he walked into the house and up the stairs to Joey's room.

Joey shut and locked the front door. Then he looked through the peephole to make sure nobody was following them. He had a reoccurring feeling of paranoia, like somebody was always following him, or his friends.

He then ran up to his room to find Henry skimming through his DVD collection which was in alphabetical order, with hundreds of movies and TV shows organized in a nifty case.

"Dude, I've never seen this one. Is it any good?" asked Henry about a horror movie called *This Will Scare You*.

"Yeah, man, actually that one is pretty damned scary. Amber and I watched it last week. It's this really freaky new-age slasher film. Half of it was shot in the first person; the other half was shot from the perspective of a dog. At the end, the dog witnesses an exorcism, but ends up saving the owner's life. Very compelling stuff."

"Sounds really trippy. Can I borrow it? I'll return it next week or something."

"That's fine. Just please don't scratch the disc. Every time I let somebody borrow a movie, I always get it back scratched up. That type of crap makes it so you can't trust anybody you know," explained Joey.

"I got you, man. I won't mess it up. I swear!"

"Okay, no problem," Joey said.

"So how's everything going with you and Amber? You guys make up since that last fight y'all had?" asked Henry.

"Fight? Hmmm... Oh, yeah, that. Bro, we've had at least three more fights since that one."

"That's not good, Joe. You have to treat her like a princess, brah! I'm telling you."

"Pshhh, what the hell do you know about relationships man? Just saying, the last girl you dated lived in Iowa, and ended up being a complete psycho!"

"When you're right, you're right," said Henry.

"Don't make me bring up the pancake incident! Or that time she came to visit you and she almost got you arrested. I'm just saying, bro, you're my friend, but also the last dude I plan on taking love life advice from."

"Geesh" said Henry.

"Again, I said no offense."

"I've learned that when somebody says 'no offense,' they are indeed going to follow it up with something offensive," said Henry.

"So, speaking of girls, any update with the Kelly twins?" asked Joey.

"Kelly twins, Kelly twins... Oh! Nahhhh. Turns out they want to have a threesome with a guy with a really good job. Like a lawyer, or a doctor, or a car salesman. Not somebody that works at a supermarket bagging groceries," explained Henry.

"Oh, yeah, because twin sisters looking for a man to have a threesome with are allowed to have that shallow of standards, huh?" Joey said sarcastically.

"Plus they are way too hot. If I were to hook up with twins, or even be involved in any form of threesome, the girls got to be like sixes, or maybe even fives. Not two dimes. I can't even comprehend sleeping with one dime, let alone two. What does the other one do when the first one's blowing me? Go on her smart phone or something?" Henry asked.

"Is that what usually happens when you're making love, dude? Do they typically pull out their cell phone?"

"I'd rather not say... but yeah, once. One time it happened. I must have not been good enough or something," said Henry with a depressed look on his face.

"Oh, shut up, man. You're a catch. Any girl would be lucky to have you," said Joey before he punched Henry in the arm.

"Hey, what the hell was that for?" he asked.

"Oh nothing. Just felt like it," Joey said, laughing.

"Dude, I forgot to ask you! Did you see those summer vacation pictures Tiffany from 10th grade drama class posted the other day on FaceSpace?"

"Dude..."

"Oh, yeah. That's right. I forgot. You are off the grid. Like some sort of social networking secret agent."

"Good one. But you know that shit's not for me" said Joey. "Got better things to do with my time then to look at pictures of food people are about to eat, or act like I like their stupid memes, random current events, Michael Johnson eating popcorn, or reading about why Monica and Jeff Fisher broke up. I really don't give a damn, man. I'd really rather do anything else, you know," Joey went on.

"Okay, okay. I get it," said Henry.

"Wait, but did you really say Tiffany from drama class? Big booty Tiffany?"

"Yes! Big booty Tiffany!"

"All right. Whatever, man, pull those damn pictures up," Joey insisted.

"I knew you would want to see 'em. Maybe you should make a FaceSpace account already."

The expression on Joey's face turned to a deeply annoyed look, "That's taking it a bit too far. Does she have some nice butt shots?"

"They were in Aruba for a week, Joey. What do you think?" asked Henry.

"Then what are we waiting for! Pull up your page already dammit!" Joey said laughing. "Get up, so I can sit down and log into FaceSpace."

"Go for it, man," said Joey, as he stood up out of his computer desk chair.

Henry sat down in the chair and spun it towards the computer. He found FaceSpace.com and logged into his account. Quickly going to his friends list, he clicked on Tiffany Lynn and pulled up her recent vacation photo album. He began scrolling to the right, skimming through all the boring pictures, until he landed on one with Tiffany in a bathing suit on the beach.

"There you go!"

"Hmmmmm...Not bad," said Joey.

"Yeah, man, and check these out," said Henry, as he kept clicking next on pictures of beautiful girls, each one a little bit more revealing than the last.

"Very nice. Thanks for showing me," said Joey, as he grabbed a movie from his DVD collection.

"See, man. Look at what you're missing not being on here," Henry said, drooling over the photos.

"I think I'll survive. Do you want to watch this movie *The Moonies*? It's like a comedy slash twisted drama combo. Very weird, but pretty interesting, if you ask me."

"Sounds good, man. I can only hang out for a little bit before I have to go to work in an hour or so."

Joey put the movie into his DVD player as the two sat back on a comfortable futon couch, arranged diagonal to his bed. Henry reached into his pocket and pulled out some weed and rolling papers. He began to break up some of it before Joey noticed him.

"Dude!!! Not in here, man! Not cool!"

Henry looked at Joey and snarled, "You know what's not cool? Not working."

"Yeah, well I got a job interview tomorrow, so stuff it."

Chapter Two
The Book of Interview

THE NEXT AFTERNOON, Joey threw on a pair of khakis and a black tennis shirt. While looking around for his new sneakers, he noticed his nametag from Mikey's Pizzeria.

"Oy, let's hope this goes better, 'k Joey?" he mumbled to himself.

He found his sneakers, put them on and made his way to the door, before tripping over a pizza box, still half full.

Joey put his hand on the doorknob and began to turn it when the door flew open and caught him on the arm and shoulder. The culprit on the other side of the door was his dad.

"Hey, son, sorry about that. Didn't see ya there," his father said, smiling.

"Yea, no shit, Dad. I was on the other side of a solid brown door. Wouldn't have guessed that you would see me."

Joey rubbed his arm and made a face that just screamed, *Thanks for solving the mystery, you warlock. Now tell me the answer to two plus two and I can die happy.*

His Dad's face suddenly went sour. "Listen, Joey. I've had a hard day, a *very* hard day at work. You've been without a job for God knows how long. How about finding one and then tell me how smart you are?"

Joey's face now said something totally different, it now said, *Yea, well guess what I'm about to tell you...you dumb ass.*

"I'm going to a job interview right now. So whenever you become a mind reader and somehow know what I'm thinking and about to do 24/7, please...feel free to let me know so I can make money off of you."

Joey smiled, and his father returned one back. They had a long history of being smart with each other on a constant basis. Joey got to his dad quite often, but they seemed to always remember that they were screwing around.

"I'll let you know how it goes, Dad."

"Can't wait to hear," said his Dad as he walked toward his bedroom after pulling another night shift.

Joey bolted back inside his room.

13

"Forgot my fucking keys," Joey said to himself, realizing he was already running late for his interview. He went through all the pockets of three pairs of dirty jeans searching for his keys. After a solid forty seconds of looking around, which of course felt more like minutes to him, he looked up at his key ring on his door to find the keys hanging right there in front of him.

Of course. The one time something's in the place that it's supposed to be in... Joey thought.

Joey grabbed his keys, headed for the door, and then went through it with purpose.

"Objective *A* accomplished: get through the damn door. Hopefully driving there and the interview won't be as challenging. If it is, I might not even make it to the interview alive for it to be bad," Joey said under his breath, mumbling.

As he made his way down the stairs and out the door, his phone rang. He looked at it as the reveal popped up on the screen. It was his other best friend, Oscar, so Joey ignored the call.

"Not even up for it right now, dude," Joey said to his phone— as if Oscar could even hear him.

Actually, he thought, as he smiled, grabbing and tilting the phone back up to his vision and tapping on Oscar's name. He hit the envelope on the phone to send Oscar a text.

It read:

> So, you going to replace that Winston Lashae DVD I let you borrow? Best stand-up comedian of all time. He can't even have every single person that comes across his DVD worship it like a newborn child. I swear, dude, did you put your blunts out on it too, Dick-head?

Joey laughed out loud, amused at his ability to send a mean text for no reason. He walked to the edge of the sidewalk where his 1996 moderately-dented blue sedan was parked and got in. He closed the door, but it got caught in his drooping seatbelt, which he yanked up before slamming the door shut. "Piece of shit car." Truth of the matter was his car wasn't even that bad, just a small dent here and there, and his seatbelt was fine. He just tended to not wind it back into place or care for the car's well-being that much.

Joey turned the ignition and the engine coughed twice but then started up. *At least, for a car from the ninety's, the engine is still in way better shape than I could hope,* Joey thought as he turned on the radio before putting the gearshift into drive to make his U-turn.

The radio was about twenty seven seconds into a hit single by a pop rock band named Fourth Dimension. The song was called "You're like No Other." Immediately he changed the station until he stumbled upon a familiar song called "Unreasonably Suspicious Cyborg" by Face Transmission.

15

"Finally! Best song of that year! Good ole' 97!" Joey said, as he began jamming in the car to his favorite song from his younger years. He made his U-Turn and headed down the street. After about seventeen seconds of driving, his phone started to beep.

"You'll have to wait until this song is over whoever you are," Joey yelled over the music blasting in his car, lying to himself because as soon as he hit a stop sign, he took his phone from a holster clipped onto his belt, for safekeeping, he would say.

It was Oscar texting back.

> Nah, but I did use it to sharpen my knife up, ya douche...really, I did. I lost a bet. Sorry dude. I'll buy you another one.

Joey started to text back, but opted not to in hopes of thinking of something mean enough to express his distaste towards his soon-to-be fallen comrade.

Letting go of the car's brake, he continued onward on his quest. He hit the gas slightly until he went through the four-way intersection, and then gave the car more gas to speed up. *Why do I...or anyone else really go slower through a four-way stop? Doesn't really help the situation at all if you think about it. Actually, it heightens your chances of getting into an accident,* Joey thought self-loathingly.

He continued to jam out to the remainder of his song, which he had downloaded to his phone previously so he could play it through the auxiliary cord at any time. He seemed to get a sense of pleasure in hearing his song live, a sense of support for his favorite band as if he hoped to get some sort of kick back from them staying tuned to their music amongst all the other choices. He frustratingly skipped through a string of songs such as "Smack Me Mama" by Brent Swords, "Honey" by Austin Owens, and "My Truck is a Real Picker Upper" by Chicken Coop Kings.

Joey turned the radio off, pissed that he never once hit another song he even remotely liked as he laid his eyes onto Burger Joint where his interview would be taking place. He slowly turned his steering wheel to the left and, in turn, made his way into the parking lot before cutting his car off in an instant in hope of saving a couple cents worth of gas.

"Here goes... something," Joey said to himself after a long sigh of dismay in response to how life seemed to be treating him. He unbuckled his seat belt, and, as always, failed to properly wind it up. He blew out a breath of air as he opened up the door. When he went to shut it, Joey, being in a hurry, didn't notice that the hinge on the seatbelt once again prevented the car door from hitting the buckle properly. He slammed the door hard after getting frustrated with the seatbelt.

Joey power-walked to Burger Joint, while tucking in the front of his shirt before heading through the door. The air was actually quite clean. Joey had heard that his acquaintance from high school, Lily Brown, had been a manager there for quite some time and had told him that she'd attempt to help him get a job there if he ever needed one.

He sat down in one of the closer-to-the-counter lobby seating booths and waited for an available manager to talk to. They were somewhat busy, so the thought that it might take a while settled into his mind rather quickly.

About twelve minutes went by. The rush had been over for about four minutes, which, of course, felt like fifteen to an anxious and nervous person awaiting an interview. Joey, bored by this point, pulled out his phone and decided to text Oscar. The text read:

> Ok, first of all, I'm taking your football card collection as collateral until you get my DVD replaced.

Joey hadn't even thought to compose a worthwhile quip to shoot at Oscar so imposing the power he had over his friend due to a classic "you owe me one" situation would have to suffice.

A few more minutes passed as Joey listened to another of his favorite bands, The Prom Sit-Outs, with headphones connected to his smart phone, as he passively expressed his discontent through his body language for the management taking their time to come see him. He had been late, after all.

Just as he figured he was too late to be interviewed and that he was being disregarded, the manager, Ms. Rebecca Shaun, came out from behind the counter.

"I almost forgot I had a four o'clock today. Well it's about four forty now, huh?" she chuckled. "No worries," she continued. "Let me grab myself a drink before we speak. Would you like something to drink?"

"A sweet tea would be great," Joey said, as he raised his left eyebrow and pressed his tongue against the left side of his cheek.

As the manager walked over to get the drinks, Joey shut off all of the apps on his phone, put it on silent, and put it in his pocket to prepare himself for the interview.

Not even ten whole seconds later, Rebecca came back with her water bottle as an associate slipped Joey his tea without him even getting a glimpse of the employee. He looked around to see who ran him the drink.

"So, what led you to want to work here?" Rebecca asked, surprising him by that question, causing him to snap into attention mode as the interview abruptly began.

"Well, I needed a job," answered Joey, with a slight smirk on his face. "It's a fast food restaurant. I mean, let's be real. Who couldn't score a job here?"

"I see," Rebecca said in a semi-monotone voice, as she jotted down some notes on a piece of paper resting on her clear blue plastic clipboard.

Joey cleared his throat rather loudly.

Rebecca then looked back at Joey, raising her head from her clipboard. "Here at Burger Joint, we believe that anyone can excel. We've opened up three new stores in this state just this past year. Would you be willing to travel to another location that the owner has if you were compensated?"

Joey's eyebrows perked up. "Yea! Ha-ha, if my car can make the trip, that is. It's old, but, it's been good thus far."

"We've all been there, trust me," she said, as she smiled. "What do you see yourself getting from this job?"

"What do you mean exactly?" Joey said.

"Do you plan on this being a career? It seems that you haven't even thought of opportunities of advancement," Rebecca continued with a blank, yet slightly shocked, expression on her face.

"Well," said Joey, "I haven't given it that much thought. I never see many guys making it to the top of these types of chains."

"That didn't exactly answer my question," said Rebecca.

"I'm sorry. I thought it definitely did," said Joey.

Rebecca looked at him with a slight grin on her face. "So, if you were to get the job..."

"Why *if*?" Joey interrupted.

Rebecca continued to ignore his cynicism. "Would you answer your phone if your, say, girlfriend texted you, while...we're in a rush?"

"I wouldn't even answer it if it was slow," said Joey, with a slight chuckle. "Hell, I wouldn't even answer it if I *wasn't* at work."

Rebecca laughed, but quickly returned back to a serious demeanor. "So, I see on your application that you were let go from your last job. What happened?"

"Well, I worked at Mikey's Pizzeria for four years. Best worker those people ever had, to be honest. But certain circumstances led me to delivering three pizzas late in the same night. Hell, it was one after the other. How were the second two possibly gonna be on time if the first one was late?"

Rebecca replied, "Yea, I sorta get that. But wha..."

"I mean, seriously," Joey interrupted once again, beginning to enrage the interviewing employer, "It's like they wanted me gone anyway. Like they set something up just to get me fired. America."

"I'm sorry to hear that. I truly hope that wasn't the case."

"Yea, like you give a rats... Anyway, sorry, go ahead."

Rebecca stared at Joey for a second, then she put her clipboard away. "Well, there are two more interviews before we decide, Mr. Taylor. But that's about it for this first interview. That's it for now. I have some things to take care of. Thanks for your time! You'll hear from us very soon."

"Wait. I was told there was only one interview for this job," Joey said, sounding surprised and annoyed.

"No, there's three. But that is none of your concern, sir."

"Yea, whatever...I knew you were going to go ahead and pull some crap on me," Joey said, angrily.

"No one's pulling anything, Mr. Taylor," Rebecca said.

"Where's Lily Brown? I need to speak to her," Joey said with a total expression of dismay.

"She doesn't work at this location anymore. She got transferred when her family moved to Cincinnati, from what I remember," Rebecca said with a slight hint of satisfaction.

Joey, seemingly panicked, went on. "Unbelievable...look, let me try this interview thing again, ma'am."

Rebecca looked at him with annoyance pretty much written across her forehead. "There's two more interviews, sir, and though you're a bit of a smart-Alek, and some of your views may be absolutely flawed and even reprehensible, that's not going to cause you to botch landing a job here. So please, have a great day and we'll contact you as soon as we're ready for your second interview. That's if we decide to give you one."

Joey stood there for a moment—a long moment—then he hocked a big gob of spit on the floor before proceeding to walk towards the door.

"OK, sir. We're going to need you to leave before we call the cops!" Rebecca exclaimed.

"I'm already heading for the door, you moron," Joey said, just loud enough for her to hear him. But Rebecca already had stormed into the office area in the kitchen and barked at an associate to go mop Joey's spit off of the floor.

I swear, people, Joey thought, as he made his way to his car. He noticed that his door wasn't shut, so he stepped into a light sprint, got to the car, and frantically looked around. Nothing seemed to be missing.

"Fuck!" he shouted to himself.

Turned out something was missing: the change that he kept in a sandwich bag in his center console was gone. It only equaled about eleven dollars, consisting of mostly quarters, nickels, a lot of dimes, and a few pennies. But this was all of his money, other than his credit card, which was already adding up to more than he could pay off.

I swear, what else can go wrong? Every little thing is just...Quit thinkin' about it, Joey! He said to himself with a frustrated tone. *There's shit you can't really do anything about!*

Joey started up his car. This time it didn't give him too much of an issue. He pulled out of the Burger Joint parking lot and sped off quickly.

*Oy, I need some gas...let the credit roll...*Joey thought.

Joey turned on the radio, but quickly tuned it out as thoughts of his day began to taunt him.

Loser Failure...

The music was phased out by a commercial, which was a lot louder than the music itself, snapping Joey out of his thoughts.

The radio host shouted out live "HEEeeeeyyyyyy, all you listeners out there in Camden County, are you ready for the free e-album giveaway? This week we're giving away ten, count them *ten* e-albs to ten lucky winners. Do you want the newest Kenny Ryan alb? Maybe your kid wants the new Tia Lisa release? Those and more artists are available! All you have to do is go on X-Soy Radio's FaceSpace page and hit *like*, and comment the answer to this question. 'What was the name of John Mills' fourth album?'"

Joey huffed, "Only my Dad would know that crap."

He drove into an open space at the Letz gas station, which was right around the corner from Burger Joint.

He turned off the car, opened the door, properly winding up his seatbelt this time. He then closed the door, feeling slightly accomplished in this small victory.

Joey began walking over to the entrance to the store when he was stopped by a younger fellow in a grey hoodie, denim jeans, and a red backwards hat.

"Hey Bruh Bruh!!!" said the young man to an infuriated Joey.

"Huh? Yeah, what can I do for you?" asked Joey, trying to make his way into the convenience store.

"Sorry to bug you man. I can see you are in a rush," the young man continued. "My name is MC Connor. I'm just out here promoting my brand new mix-tape!"

The young charismatic rapper reached out his hand to give Joey dap. Joey shook his hand and looked at the door of the gas station, tempted to just go get his ice-cold Mountain Mist slushie.

"Oh, yeah. That's pretty cool," said Joey in an almost sarcastic tone.

"Yea, man. Take a listen to this track called Kill Shit Daily. This is one of my favorites. Everybody's telling me it's pretty dope."

MC Connor took his ear buds off and insistently held them out to Joey who put them in his ears.

Joey listened for about thirty seconds, as MC Connor bobbed his head next to him and smiled, looking for a sign of approval from a disgruntled Joey who was just trying to get out of the conversation. The music was actually pretty good, thought Joey, and on a better day and time, he would probably have been interested in socializing with a local aspiring rapper like him.

He wasn't particularly too into rap, but he had gone through phases where he listened to it quite often in the past. Not too much as of late though, and as Joey listened to it a bit more, MC Connor bobbed his head back and forth to his own beat he could hear coming out of the other side of the headphones.

Joey took the ear buds off and gave them back to the young aspiring emcee.

"Thanks, man. It's pretty good. I can't lie. You got some decent flow and lyrics, but I'm pretty broke right now, and I don't want to offend you or nothing, but I got to go inside. I'm sort of in a rush," said Joey, as he gave MC Connor back the headphones and began walking to the door.

"Hey man. I appreciate you taking a second to talk at all," said MC Connor.

Joey stopped and looked back and saw the MC was holding out a CD.

"Here, Bruh, take one please. I'm tryna sell them for five bucks a pop. But if you can't afford it, at least take one and try to spread the word for me, fam. I'm tryna blow up ya know what I mean?" said the friendly rapper.

Joey took the gift and looked at the front of the cheap CD case. On the cover was a cartoon of a fierce lion holding an Uzi, and the words: "MC Connor: Yo Bitch My Bish" with a URL at the bottom that read facespace.com/MCConnor.

"Cool. If it's free, sure, I'll take it man. Thanks," said Joey as he went to high five MC Connor.

The rapper high fived him back before he threw his backpack over his head and said "I'm gonna pray for you, fam. I hope you pray for me na'mean," said MC Connor.

"I know what you mean," said Joey as he started to laugh and continued to walk into the Letz gas station.

"Don't ever sell out, kid" said Joey as he opened the door.

"I got you, bruh!" said MC Connor.

Joey arrived back home about a half hour later, walked through the front door and stomped his way upstairs to his room. His mother shouted "Hey honey" but Joey ignored her and slammed his door shut.

He reached his hand into his pocket and pulled out the CD MC Connor had given him. He looked at it and thought, *hm, maybe I should listen to this. It sounded pretty good in his headphones.*

But laziness came over Joey before he tossed the rapper's mixtape into a hamper full of dirty clothes that had been piling up for weeks in the corner of his room.

Maybe another time, he thought as he lay down on his bed, grabbed the remote control and turned on his 32" flat screen television to watch his favorite crime show, *TSI: Sexual Predator Unit.*

Chapter Three
The Book of Monty's

THE NEXT DAY, Joey slept in after staying up until 5 a.m. At first, he applied to jobs online, from clothing stores to various restaurants. He finally got bored, as well as slightly discouraged. Most of the jobs he had found, he wasn't qualified for, but that didn't stop him from applying. It soon dawned on him that he might not be qualified for any job that was not fast food or retail. And after his most recent interview, Joey started to feel that he wasn't even able to keep his anger in check long enough to get a job to work fast food.

Once he gave the applications a break, he turned to ViewTube to keep him entertained for a few hours before ultimately crashing.

He tossed and turned in his bed before fully waking up. Joey looked at his alarm clock and saw that it was already 2:33 p.m. *Oh shit,* he thought to himself.

Joey finally rolled out of bed in nothing but his boxers and realized his phone was lit up with 14 missed calls.

Amber called 12 times, and he also got 2 missed calls from Oscar. *This girl is freaking nuts,* Joey thought to himself.

Joey then saw she had messaged him six times, with messages that read "WAKE UP!! WAKE UP!!!!" and "We are supposed to go out to lunch," as well as many more. But he just deleted the rest because he could imagine what they all said.

His phone began vibrating in his hand, and it was Amber again. "Great," Joey said to himself before he answered the call.

"Heyyyyy" Joey said, putting the phone up to his ear.

"Where the hell are you?" asked Amber.

"I just woke up. Chill out." Joey moved the phone away from his mouth, so he could yawn and then wiped the boogers out of his eyes.

"Well, sooooo sooooorrrrrrryyyyyy to wake you up," Amber said.

"Look, I was up late applying for jobs," Joey said.

"Well that's good at least," Amber responded.

"Yeah, it is what it is."

"I still haven't eaten lunch. Will you get dressed and come meet me at Monty's BBQ? I got an hour until I have to be back to work. We have a big meeting at 4 o'clock with some investors," she went on.

"Yeah, that's fine. I'll be there in ten minutes," said Joey.

"All right, babe. I'll see you soon," Amber said before she hung up.

After the call ended, Joey threw on some dirty khakis and a green shirt. He slipped into his trusty white sneakers and ran out of the house without even brushing his teeth. Already late, he didn't want to make his girlfriend even angrier. She had a temper that he tried to keep stored away for a rainy day.

After speeding up the road, trying to make every green light, Joey finally pulled up to the BBQ restaurant, where his girlfriend was pacing back and forth in front of the entrance, waiting for him. *Oh no, she's going to be pissed I can already tell*, he thought.

"Hey, glad you can make it!" said Amber, with what seemed to be a smug attitude, before rolling her eyes, as she opened the door to Monty's BBQ.

Monty's was known for its smoked beef brisket and pulled pork sandwiches. Every Wednesday, pulled pork sandwiches were only $5.99, and came with cornbread, one side, and a drink. Not a bad deal in comparison to most restaurants. Amber and Joey ate there a couple times a month on average.

They walked to their favorite booth near the far right corner. Joey followed Amber in to sit next to her, rather than across from her. She gave him a look of surprise, as she parked her purse in between the two of them, creating separation, and giving Joey the feeling that she was upset with him. But then she confused him by grabbing his hand and picking up the menu.

"So, what do you want to eat, babe? I'm starving. Haven't had a bite to eat since a green apple this morning when I woke up," said Amber, looking over the menu.

"I'm feeling like getting some BBQ brisket and chicken, if that's okay with you," said Joey, feeling a bit petty and embarrassed.

"That's fine, Joseph. I told you I got you covered until you get your next job, all right?"

A short skinny waiter walked over with a pen and small pad and said, "How we doing guys? My name's Pete. I will be your waiter today."

"We're fine. Thanks," said Joey.

"Can I start you two off with anything to drink?" asked Pete the waiter.

"Yeah, I'll take a water," said Amber.

"I will take a Mountain Mist, little ice," said Joey.

"I'm sorry sir, we no longer carry that beverage. We only have Sprits, or Ray's Cola products," the waiter went on.

"Ughh, I guess I'll just take a water then," said a frustrated Joey.

"All right. I'll get that right out to you, guys, and I'll give you a couple minutes to look over what you want to eat."

Pete walked to the back to get their drinks.

"No Mountain Mist? This place officially sucks," said Joey.

Amber gripped his hand tighter. "Water is better for you anyway. You don't need all those wasted calories. You already drink like five of those a day. I'm surprised your teeth haven't rotted yet."

They looked over the menu for a minute or two before Pete the waiter came back over with their waters.

"Have you guys decided what you want yet?"

"Yea, I guess. I think I'll take the BBQ chicken and brisket meal, with macaroni and cheese, mashed potatoes, and corn bread," said Joey.

"Excellent choice" said the waiter. "And you ma'am?"

"I will take the pulled pork sandwich special, with potato salad, coleslaw, and cornbread. Mayonnaise on the side please," said a hungry Amber.

"Also an excellent choice. I'll have those right out for you two."

The waiter picked up the menus and specials and headed to the back to put in the order.

"Sooooo, the other day I was thinking about something... and promise me you won't get mad when I say this," Amber paused.

"But?" asked a paranoid Joey.

"Well, all my friends... like Tina, Melissa, Jennifer, pretty much all of them. Their FaceSpace pages say they are in a relationship with their boyfriends."

"Okay...?"

"Well, mine just says "in a relationship," but with nobody," said Amber.

"Well you're in a relationship with me," Joey responded.

"They don't know that!" she said.

"Who the hell is 'they'?" asked Joey.

"You know, *people*. Like my friends, my classmates, my co-workers, my family! Everybody that I know, Joseph," she said.

"Oh. I see. Well, I'm sorry, Hun. But you know I don't use that FaceSpace crap," said Joey.

"Yes, I am well aware. You are the only person I know that refuses to make a FaceSpace page. The only problem with the whole thing, Joseph, is that you are my boyfriend. I want to be able to show you off to everyone. And I can't even tag you in my photos.

Do you know how much that sucks?"

"No, not really," Joey replied.

"For all you know, every guy in the damn county could be sending me pictures of their junk and telling me how gorgeous I am every day, and you would never even know, Joey."

"Well, that wouldn't be cool," Joey said, laughing.

"Shut up! I'm serious!"

Amber's shouting made the other six people in the restaurant turn their heads to the couple's table.

"Listen, Hunny, I'm sure if you had a problem with some guy trying to hit on you or whatever you would take care of it, and if it got really bad, I'm sure you would tell me. Wouldn't you?"

"That's not the point. I just want you on there with me. I want people to know who my damn boyfriend is. Is that too much to ask?"

"Look, I have been off the grid for a while now, and I don't plan on giving into society's plan of conforming everybody to a damned computer, where the government and corporate industries can see your whereabouts at all times, see what you search for, your interests, and then bombard you with advertisements until you pay for some product from one of their sponsors that you probably won't ever actually need. I'm sorry I won't give into the system, sweetie."

"Ugh," said his angered girlfriend.

"Look. I haven't had an account on any of those sites in forever. Matter of fact, I haven't had one since the last big thing everybody used, MyFace, and that was at least cool. You were able to rank your best friends in order from 1-8, and the government didn't invade your space and privacy every chance they got," said Joey.

"Well I'm not going to keep bringing this up with you. I know you like to be anti-social, and I won't be able to change that. I'm sorry. I just want people to know that somebody out there loves me." Amber pulled out her phone to check her FaceSpace like she did everywhere they went.

After some time, Pete the Waiter walked from around the corner, holding a carrying tray with both of their BBQ dishes steaming hot, out from the kitchen, smelling magnificent. The meat smoker in the back of the restaurant left a sting in your nose that would last until you went to sleep.

"Why, thank you." said Amber, as Pete placed her plate in front of her. He then gave Joey his dish as he asked, "Is there anything else I can get for you two?"

"Yes. Do you guys have that tangy spicy BBQ sauce in the

back?" asked Joey.

"I will bring some right out to you, sir," said Pete before he ran to the back to grab a squeeze bottle of one of their famous BBQ sauces. He came back to the table and handed Joey the exquisite sauce.

"Thank you so much. Everything looks so great," said Amber, as she began digging into her coleslaw, and then spreading her mayonnaise on the BBQ pulled pork sandwich. When both sides were covered, she took her first bite of the large sandwich. "Mmmmmmm," she said, as she swallowed her food. "Soooo good."

Damn. Can she chew her food any louder? Joey thought to himself.

"What was that?" said Amber as she continued to stuff her face with her Pulled Pork.

Oh shit. Did I say that out loud? I need to think more quietly, Joey thought.

"Nothing, Hun. How's your sandwich?"

"Amazing," said Amber, as she kept tearing up her food.

"Good," said Joey as he took a bite out of his BBQ chicken. *Mmmmm this is good,* he thought.

"Oh, so like I was saying," said Amber. "Have you ever considered even making a FaceSpace account? It's not like you have to use it all the time. But at least to check it once in a while."

"Hmmm, actually, now that I think about it, when they first created FaceSpace, I did make an account. I turned out not to like it. Became very lame to me, very quickly," said Joey, as he took a bite of his mashed potatoes, followed by some macaroni and cheese.

"Oh, what a shame. If only I had dated you then, huh?" Amber said, sarcastically.

"Actually, right before I deactivated my account, I remember I made a joke celebrity page, for God," said Joey. "I thought it would be funny to see if anybody would "like" it. Unfortunately I only got like 133 followers or something."

Amber started to laugh before she took a sip of her ice water. "Oh really, now?"

"Yeah, I mean. I'm a rebel, you know. I don't care what people think. I thought it would be funny. Too bad it didn't catch on, you know," he said.

"Hmm, you said that was how long ago?" asked Amber.

"Umm, probably about four years ago" said Joey.

"Well, have you checked it at all recently?" Amber asked.

"Na, I don't log onto that lame crap," he said, laughing. "Why would I?"

"Well, at least you were having fun. Plus your girlfriend wants you to have a FaceSpace so she can 'Nudge' you all day. Plus maybe your blasphemous page has new followers," she said before taking a bite into her potato salad.

"Oh yeah? I doubt it. I'm sure there are tons of other pages for God already. Nobody is gonna follow mine, which hasn't been active in four years, let alone ever. I'd be surprised if it hasn't been deleted by now," said Joey.

"That's pretty funny. You should check if it's still out there. I bet your 133 followers are waiting on you to make your return!" Amber laughed, as she wiped off her cheek with a napkin.

"Naaaa, I'm good. Maybe if I get really bored one day, but yeah, I still doubt it. That shit's lame."

They both dug into their food again, spending most of the rest of their time at Monty's BBQ eating in silence and very quickly too since Amber had to get back to work soon.

Chapter Four
The Book of Tyson

AFTER HIS LATE LUNCH WITH AMBER, Joey pulled up in front of Oscar's house, where he, Henry, Oscar, and two other friends, Cody and Chris, had made plans to get together and hang out.

Oy, time to waste some time with these silly dudes. I bet they're playing video games, drinking beer, and probably thinking of doing some unnecessary drug, Joey thought, as he turned off his car.

Joey got out of his sedan and headed for the door. He knocked on the door, causing it to swing open. Someone must have not closed it all the way, as usual.

"Of course," Joey sighed to himself, as he walked into Oscar's house.

"Guys!" Joey screamed out in hopes of someone hearing him over the loud music.

No one answered, so Joey decided to follow the music. It led him to the basement. He opened the door and was nearly knocked on his bottom by the amount of smoke that came out of the room.

Fanning the smoke away from his face, Joey entered the room, where, sure enough, they were playing video games. Soccer Pro, to be exact. They were also surrounded by more open beer cans than one could count. Cody was on the couch packing a two foot plastic bong with some Mello Mango Kush he had been bragging about all week.

Joey smirked at the thought that he was 100% dead-on with his cynical assumptions about his closest friends. Oscar quickly got up from sitting next to Cody and greeted Joey.

"Hey dude! What's up? It's about time you got here. How was lunch with Amber or whatever you had to do?"

"Lunch was fine. Where are those football cards so I can burn... I mean keep them until you replace my DVD."

"Hrmph, really, man? Come on, Joe. I'll replace it. I know it was stupid, but..."

"Yes, it was stupid," Joey interrupted. "Now I'm doing the smart thing by taking those cards. Now, make with em' duders. Make with them."

Oscar headed out of the room muttering obscenities.

"Cooooooooooooody" Joey said. "What's up, man?

Cody, who had packed four different bongs, grabbed a cold Queen Cougar Light and threw it towards Joey, who simply shifted to the left, allowing the beer can to fly past him and hit the floor, spraying beer everywhere. Joey perked his lips and nodded his head as if to say "good job." Cody then ran over to grab a towel to clean up the mess.

"You guys still hiring over at Great Purchase?" asked Joey. "I haven't worked retail in forever, and I miss the hell out of it. Besides, working fast food really wasn't cutting it."

Cody answered, "They are, sort of, I guess. I'd fill out an application. But they're kinda giving a lot of people the run around right now. So I wouldn't get too excited the way things are goin', to be real. I don't even know how much longer I'll be there."

His phone rang, and Cody answered, while plugging his free ear with his other hand so he could hear over the noise.

"Hey there, Mr. Jodes," said Cody, putting his finger to his mouth, indicating everyone should be quiet. Mr. Jodes was Cody's manager at Great Purchase.

"I'm sorry. Did you say I'm fired?" asked Cody, still trying to tune his ears for optimum clarity.

"Say what? LOL. Oh, I've been fired up!" Cody laughed out loud. "Seriously? Thank you, Sir. I won't let you down."

Cody hung up the phone with a big smile on his face.

"What, your boss ripped you a new one about your job?" Joey asked.

"No, man. I just got a promotion to Sales Lead!" He grabbed a bong. "I'll smoke one to that shit!"

Oscar came stumbling through the door holding a laminated binder full of football cards.

"Here ya go, you asshole," said Oscar. "That's at least ten thousand dollars' worth of cards. Please don't let anything happen to them."

"Dude, I was just screwing with you. Keep your corny ass football cards. Just give me $25 to replace my DVD, and we'll call it a day. Be happy I'm not charging you for the gas I had to waste just to get it again."

"God! Thank you, Joey! Freakin' cocksucker."

Oscar quickly ran back towards the door to return his prized cards to their home on his dresser.

"So what's he playing," asked Joey. "Soccer Pro? Why won't he just get his lazy ass up and play an actual game of soccer instead? I swear, video games are gonna turn America into the single laziest country of all time, if it isn't already."

He went over to the mini cooler to grab himself a drink. "Jeez, finally...a fuckin' Mountain Mist."

He chugged it as if it was going to rot. It had been a solid day since he felt the sensation of his favorite beverage.

Just then, the door swung open and a Hispanic guy (awkward) ran in and busted out a nifty backhand spring for no apparent reason and screamed, "Tyson's here, bitches!"

A cluster mix of "heys and yeah's" greeted Tyson's arrival. Tyson, full-blown Peruvian, was well-known for being the life of any and every party he attended. He had two brothers, Darius and Andrew, who died with their father in an airplane crash while visiting their old residence in Lima, Peru. He then began living by the philosophy that you only have one life, so live it up and be the life of the party at any and every opportunity. He never went against his wacky philosophies.

"Freakin' Miguel, howzit goin' man," said Joey.

"Jajajaja, it's Tyson, you racist prick. Now come here and give me a hug," Tyson said, as he brought him in for a tight one.

Joey welcomed the embrace, as Tyson was the one he liked the most, even slightly more than his best friend, Oscar. At least, he respected Tyson more.

"So how's your mom, man? I freakin' miss Mrs. Mendez," said Joey, as the embrace came to an end.

"She's doing awesome, man," Tyson explained. "She just got her Associates after not being able to pay her college debt for like, nine years. It's nuts. She majored in psychology. Now she's working as a social worker at Harver Jerome Prince Middle School. She's finally able to pay those damn past due medical bills, and she's been feeling better, of course. Less stress helps as well. You know how that is. I've been looking for work myself. I have some money saved up so I'm straight, but still...I don't need that going away either," said Tyson, as he picked up an unopened beer, and cracked it open before taking a large gulp.

"Hell, man, that's awesome, du...-"

Joey was interrupted by Oscar coming back into the room before he jumped on Tyson for a hug. Tyson quickly pushed off Oscar, who smelled heavily of alcohol.

"Hey man! How's your Mom?" asked Oscar.

Tyson, not willing to repeat everything he just said, simply replied, "She's good, bro. How's your aunt, with that sexy ass of hers? She upstairs?"

"She's just fine. Yeah, she's upstairs with her boyfriend. You gonna try and pry her away? I'd love to see that shit. That dude is buff as fuck."

"Well, you know what I always say, bro, Tyce will *always roll the dice*!"

Tyson was joined by literally everyone in the end of his corny but ever-so-popular catchphrase. Joey shook his head as a spurt of laughter spit escaped his lips. "You guys are too fuckin' hilarious," said Joey.

"You think it's a joke?" Tyson exclaimed, as he headed out the door to try his hand at wooing Oscar's aunt, Erica. "I'm hittin' the stairs NOW!"

"So...how is it rooming with your aunt?" asked Joey, "I know you both needed each other bad. Especially after her dumb ass boyfriend lost all that money in Atlantic City."

"You say that every time you come over here, bro," Oscar said, as he picked up a Queen Cougar Light for a sip.

"Never stopped being true," Joey quipped with a snide smirk growing across his face.

Oscar took $25 from his pocket, mockingly wiped his ass with it, and handed it to Joey.

Joey reluctantly accepted the money he was owed, turned around, and then back around slowly. He then began grinding his shoe into Oscar's brand new pair of Jayman's. "Are we done being four year old assholes now?"

"Touché', my friend, touché. Can't say I didn't deserve that one. Now get off." Oscar shoved Joey off.

"Hey guys! Who's ready to get in on these bong hits?" asked Cody.

I gotta get out of here, Joey thought.

"I'll grab Tyson," said Joey. "I'm sure he'll want to get in on this."

As Joey headed upstairs to find Tyson, in the background, he heard a voice that he was sure to be Chris's screaming "Where all the hoes at?"

Joey chuckled to himself, as he headed into the living room area where he saw Tyson speaking to Aunt Erica and her boyfriend about the benefits of an open relationship.

"It promotes the instincts of a man and woman that tells them 'I want to cheat.' You know what that is?" asked Tyson, smiling.

Randy, Erica's boyfriend uttered, "Yo, you're two seconds away from getting knocked out."

"Don't be rude," said Tyson. "It's called exercising variety. You get bored with each other and break up. If you spread your win ..."

"Okkaaaaaay!" Joey Interrupted. "Dude, they're doing bong hits, man, they need you down there. Plus, Cody got a promotion, so it's probably going to turn into a mad house."

"Bet, homie, bet bet *bet*!" Tyson yelled as he started to run towards the basement door.

Joey then turned to Erica and her boyfriend and said, "You weren't buying that bullshit, were you Erica?"

He soon got bored with the party, and quietly made his exit with the stealth movements of a secret agent.

Joe arrived back at his house before 10:30 p.m. and made his way up to his room to take a seat in front of his computer. He immediately went to ViewTube to watch its latest original series, *The Hand That Kills*, a show about a spirit that possesses hands and causes them to commit murder. Joey thought the idea was ridiculous, but the show entertained him so much he watched it on a weekly basis.

Just then his phone dinged. It was Amber shooting him a text. He paused the show.

The text read:

Hey babe! I know you don't have a FaceSpace, so I thought I'd be the first to make you laugh. You know Oscar's aunt, of course. She and Tyson just became friends on the site. Too funny, right?

Joey texted back

> LOL

Although, he was not in fact laughing out loud at all. He went on to type:

> That's too funny. That kid is something else. Far too much charisma for any one man.

He clicked on *play* to resume his show, but seconds, later his phone dinged again.

Amber's text read:

> Tyson is such a freak! He's a real sweetheart though, plus what you told me about her boyfriend and the gambling? Fuck that guy.

Joey replied with an agreeable:

> Yeah

in an effort to make it difficult for her to respond, at least right away.

His phone dinged again anyway.

Damn it, Amber, he thought, as he picked up his phone.

Only this time it was Oscar, so Joey just ignored the text. Then, as he was about to click on his show to escape reality for a moment, his phone rang. It was Oscar again. Joey was annoyed, but decided to pick up the phone, knowing his friend wouldn't stop bothering him until he answered.

"Hey man, you dipped out! What gives?" asked Oscar.

"It was mad smoky down there, man, first off. Secondly, it was about to get a lot smokier."

"Bro, you're the biggest buzzkill on the face of this planet. Have some fun, man. Loosen up!"

"I would have fun if all of my friends weren't a bunch of burn-outs that have to play video games all day to escape their reality, smoke pot all the time to forget their reality even exists, and drink beer to enjoy themselves. If it were done in some sort of moderation I could at least chill you know? Maybe smoke outside so I don't have to like die in there."

"Hell, man. There's no video games outside," explained Oscar.

"Thanks for proving my point."

"I STILL SEE NOT A SINGLE BITCH!" Chris cried out in the background.

"That's funny. Yo, Chris is fuckin' hilarious. Is he doing a handstand now? I'm sure he's wasted, blasted, and everything in between."

Oscar turned around to look at Chris who was actually on the floor squirming up and down. He turned back around and put the phone back to his ear. "Nope, he's not doing a handstand. Why won't you come back, man? Just have one drink with us. And you really have to see Chris's interpretation of the Worm."

"Dude, just drop it, all right? Why do you guys need alcohol to have a good time? Why do you have to be drunk? Why do you need drugs to feel good? Why do you need video games all the time? What's wrong with the people around you and interacting? Can you answer a single one of those questions? If you can, I'll play a video game, drink a beer, *and* smoke a bong with you guys."

"Uhhhhh..."

"Thought not," said Joey. Hey, man, I gotta go, ok? I'm watching the new episode of *That Hand That Kills*, I'm gonna find out if Ashton survived that ridiculous shoot out at the Clam Station.

"Whatever, Mr. Killjoy. We'll be over here, havin' fun without you," said Oscar.

In the background, Chris yelled out, "Yo, tell Joey he's a lil bitch for leaving! We need all the bitches we can get here!"

"Night, you guys. Enjoy yourselves," said Joey.

Joey hung up before Oscar could get his farewell out and quickly clicked on the show he was watching before something else would interrupt him.

He was watching intently as he took a sip from his Mountain Mist. Suddenly, a hand reached out from the darkness and grabbed the heroine, causing Joey to jump back and cough up his soda all over his 22-inch computer monitor. As he recovered from the cough, he quickly ran downstairs and to the kitchen, grabbed some paper towels, and returned to his room to soak up the soda he sprayed onto his computer.

Now where in this video was I at? Joey thought, as he clicked back about thirty seconds. Just as he found the right spot, the phone rang again. This time, it was Amber.

"Hey, baby. I know you were out with your friends tonight. I'm watching a movie with my mom. I started to think about you. I just wanted to say that I love you and hope you're doing all right. You seemed a bit agitated when I was texting you earlier," said Amber.

"No, I'm just tired of hearing about FaceSpace. Everyone is on it all the time. Everyone talks about it all the time. Did people forget that someone is like, sitting or standing right in front of them? I mean...God that's annoying.

"Stop using the Lord's name in vain young man."

"Yeah. And that too. Every time I say 'God' in another way other than singing his praises, I hear the same thing from everyone, like a bunch of robots. 'Don't say the Lord's name in vain.' I'm sure half the people that say it don't even know what 'in vain' means. People need to think for themselves, for once," he replied.

"Well, I do agree with you there baby. But I know what 'in vain' means, so I'm not one of them."

"Oh really? What does it mean then?"

There's a bit of a pause.

"You're looking it up, aren't you?"

"Dammit, you caught me."

Chapter Five
The Book of FaceSpace

THE NEXT MORNING, Joey opened his eyes and slid into consciousness. It was 7:23 a.m. He sat up and let out a big yawn before pivoting on his backside to step out of the bed.

Man...another day, thought Joey, as he put on the same socks he wore the day before. He then slid on some sweatpants, threw on an orange sleeveless shirt, and headed to his computer chair.

Joey first clicked on Findoo.com and searched for more jobs that were hiring in the area. As he skimmed through the job postings, he noticed the Burger Joint ad was still up.

Pssh, yeah okay, Joey thought, as he continued to scroll down the page. He saw a 'Help Wanted' ad for a programmer for

FaceSpace. "Ugh," he sighed out loud.

Joey immediately sprung out of the chair and headed downstairs to grab himself something to eat from the kitchen, *Chimichanga's sounds good,* as he grabbed one from the freezer.

He could hear his phone ringing from upstairs as he threw his food into the microwave and set the time for a minute and forty five seconds. He headed back up towards his room, taking his time, in hopes that he'd miss the phone call. It was Amber. He texted her back:

> Hey babe, about to eat right now, what's up?

The phone rang again. It was Amber of course. This time, he answered it.

"Hey jerk-face! You think I care if you're eating!? Don't answer that. I just wanted to tell you that I'm going to be at my brother's baseball game all morning so if you text me or call and I don't answer, that's why."

"No problem, Jerk...ier, face."

Joey scratched his ear in disbelief that he couldn't come up with a better comeback. It was early, after all.

"Look, babe, I love you, k? I'll keep myself entertained," he said.

"You better. Just behave!"

"I will, dearest. Been looking up applications. So far your beloved FaceSpace seems to have more jobs available than the real world does."

"Joey, FaceSpace *is* the real world, just like everything else. It connects people better than anything ever has. I wish you'd give it a chance...anyway, I have to finish getting ready. I love you, hun."

"I guess I see what you mean, in a way, and I love you too. Have fun watching your, ah, sports."

They hung up, and Joey was back to his lonely state of existence. He found a few more places that were hiring, but all of them were set up directly through FaceSpace. So Joey decided to put his job search on hold a while and switched his attention to ViewTube.

He sifted through some of the original programming they had online. Since he'd been out of work for about three months, he got into the habit of binge watching a lot of the shows he was currently into.

*Wow, I've never been so bored...*Joey thought, as he constantly navigated between the 'Tab of Employment' and the 'Tab of Enjoyment' on his web browser.

"Whatever," sighed Joey. "Might as well go on FaceSpace and

make a FaceSpace page so I can at least apply for one of these jobs," he said out loud to himself with the aim of a solid motivational push from within.

Reluctantly, Joey typed in the letters 'F-A-C-E-S-P-A-C-E-.-C-O-M' into his browser bar. The FaceSpace website popped up on his screen.

I never thought I'd see this page open again.

Joey moved the mouse pointer to the register link. The thought of making a FaceSpace page caused him to freeze. *Is this really worth it? If my God page only got a hundred or so followers, what's it really going to do for me?*

So before he clicked on the register link, he remembered Amber's question from the other night: "Maybe your blasphemous page has some new followers?"

He then moved the cursor upwards and into the sign-in area, clicked on the e-mail box and entered his e-mail address and password, causing his page for 'God' to pop up on the right side of the home screen. The profile picture was of a cartoon drawing of some random Internet artist's depiction of "God" that Joey had found on Findoo years ago when he had originally created the page out of boredom. He noticed the site had changed a lot since the last time he was on FaceSpace four years before. He didn't know what to put for the 'cover photo' as a banner that went across the page.

Joey laughed and said to himself, "Well, this is pretty silly." He scrolled down the page until he came to something that couldn't possibly be right. Above his location read 31.4M Followers.

"What in the holy hell," he said aloud. "Ooops, sorry, God." But what does 31.4 M mean? Did I lose a hundred followers? And how can there be point-four of a follower. And what's that *M* mean? Oh wait. Here it is."

Joey looked down at an asterisk at the bottom of the page, where next to the asterisk was the letter *M*, and next to it the word *million.*

Suddenly, Joey's face lit up, and his heart began to beat 10 times faster in his chest.

"This can't be. Thirty-one point four million followers? There's no freaking way."

This can't be real. How the hell is this even possible?

As he navigated the page some more, his jaw dropped open even wider. He truly could not believe it.

He clicked on the list of followers, and the list went on and on and on. Joey clicked on a few profiles of his followers to investigate them and find out if they were real and not just bots of some sort. Joey thought they may have been fake followers because he had heard about certain celebrities paying for likes and followers before. The pages checked out and had all been updated that day with photos, statuses, check-ins, tags, etc.

This is outstanding. Maybe FaceSpace isn't really all that bad. Wait till the boys see this, Joey thought.

He scrolled down to his ShareWall, which read "No Posts Made Yet." He moved the cursor over to the tab on the side that had his Messages, which indicated 1000 plus.

"Wow! Some people have a lot of time on their hands huh?" Joey spun his computer chair around and looked at himself in the mirror and began to laugh.

Well, still, at least when I have time on my hands, I make it useful! He rolled his eyes, as he went back to open up a few messages.

There were a few spam messages from different companies, non-profit organizations, clothing lines. Even Ray's Cola and Mountain Mist had various messages sent to the "God" page Joey had created. He continued to scroll down to find real messages from some real people. Joey opened up one message from one person named Jack Jackson.

The boy in the profile picture looked no older than fourteen, which meant that technically he wasn't even supposed to be on the social networking site. Joey laughed and said, "Let's see what Jack

Jackson wants with God."

The message was sent at 10:24 P.M on Tuesday, June 24th. Joey read it out loud.

"Dear God,

I know you haven't been very active on here and I believe that is because you are busy watching over all of us, including my Mama, my brother Jerry, and sister Leslie. We lost my father last year and things have been really tough. I just wanted to reach out to you and ask you to bless me and my family. We need the strength to go on through these tough times. Bless my mother as she has been so strong since we lost papa.

I haven't felt much love from you lately, but I know you are still up there watching out for us good people out here that never did nothing wrong to anybody. All the bad things I've stayed away from and I still have my Daddy taken away from me, I don't think that's fair. But you must have a plan for all of us and I know if I keep praying and believing in you, u will lead us to the better days ahead of us. I just can't see them right now. Thank you God. I love you God. Amen.

From,
Jack"

As Joey read this out loud at his computer desk, he couldn't help but feel pity for the high school kid that had messaged his God page, a page that hadn't ever been updated.

Joey did not know how to react to that initial message, so he continued to look over the others that came from all sorts of people from all over the world, of all genders, races, religions, and ages. He scrolled far down past hundreds of unopened mail to one message sent two years prior. It was from a Lucy Williams. This one caught his attention as he opened up the message. He decided to click on her account because she looked very pretty in her profile picture. Before reading the message, he zoomed in closer on a few of the more flattering pictures on her profile page. Joey was in a semi state of shock at how beautiful she was. *Now this is what I want to see. What do you want from me?* Joey thought, as he continued to study her page to find out a little bit more about Lucy. She was eighteen years old, from Los Angeles, California, studying to be a biochemist, and worked at a nail salon in the meantime. It said she was 'in a relationship' with a guy named Paul Richmond.

Paul looks like a little dick asshole if you ask me, Joey thought, as a bit of jealousy rained over him as his interest in Lucy had dropped a tad.

He continued back to her message, sent at 3:38 P.M on Friday, April 2nd. The message read...

"To My Heavenly Father,

Why does my boyfriend have to lay his hands on me? Why do I deserve this treatment, God? Paul use to be such a nice guy and now when he gets drunk, and we start to fight...he starts to push me. Last week he slapped me across the face, left a mark under my eye. I had to lie to my job when they asked what happened.

I know there is somebody good inside of him. I fell in love with him last year and I never thought he would end up like this. But last night, after a bottle of Russian Vodka, Paul hit me three times, once in the face, twice in the stomach. It hurt so bad. God, please send me a sign, or please save me from the man he is becoming. I don't want to leave him. But I don't know what to do. Please send me a sign, God.

Lucy"

"Whoa!" Joey said to himself. "That's fucked up!"

Joey read a few more messages in astonishment. He had no idea how to react to this new-found "online fame," or better yet, infamy.

After he got tired of reading dozens of messages from all sorts of people, he was still amazed. He had no idea this was possible and had no idea about what to do with his page for "God."

He exited out of FaceSpace and went to his DVD collection. He picked one of his favorite television shows, *Karma* Season Two, and popped it into his DVD player, then jumped on his bed and laid back on his pillow.

The show started, but Joey couldn't get God's FaceSpace page out of his head. He couldn't help but think of what he should do. He started watching the first episode, hoping to get sucked into the T.V show. It didn't work.

"I am God," said Joey to himself. "No, that's not right. That sounds so weird. But I *am* the creator of the Creator's FaceSpace page. That's a little better."

Joey's cell phone vibrated in his pocket. At first it scared him, thinking it might be some kind of sign for having such thoughts. He pulled it out of his sweatpants and looked at the screen. He had received a text message from Oscar that read:

> Watchu Up To, Pussy???!

He began to type back faster than he had ever typed before:

> DuUUUde. You have no idea what just happened to me man!

He clicked *send*.

Thirty seconds later, he got a text back from Oscar that read

> What happened??? Did Amber dump your broke ass yet? Hahahah!

Not even, Dick. I can't even type all this out my dude. Come over? I'll tell you in person. It's pretty damned crazy

I'll be there in an hour or so. Needa get some gas

Oh okay, you're stopping at Letz? Can you get me a Mountain Mist dude? I'll pay you when you get here

Naaaaa, not a gas station. I needa get some gassssss. You know. Kushhh. Dro. Oh yeah, I forgot you're no fun and don't know dick about shit. LOLOLOL

I forgot, ya pot head

Joey sent back to Oscar.

See ya in a bit

texted Oscar.

Oscar is not gonna believe this, thought Joey. *Nobody is.*

Some time passed, and he still couldn't get it out of his mind how crazy it is that more than 31 million people had liked his "God" page over the past few years. He wanted to text Amber, but decided he'd wait until she came over to surprise her with it.

It's like people somehow believed that God was reintroduced to the world through social media and FaceSpace. Ironically, it made plenty of sense. Pop stars, political figures, all of these so-called 'idol's' are gods in their own minds and in the minds of their fans, or fanatics with extreme enthusiasm for religion and politics.

Joey wondered would that mean that because he controlled this page, that he *was* God? He wondered what possible power or control come could from this.

About forty minutes later, Oscar started throwing rocks at Joey's window. He shot Oscar a text that read

> Hey man, I left all the doors unlocked, come on up

Two minutes later, Oscar appeared in Joey's room.

"Welcome, man. You just missed about six of my birthday parties, but...welcome," Joey said, sarcastically.

"My bad. I was watching a video when you texted me. I swear, you can find anything on ViewTube," Oscar laughed. "Wanna watch?"

"Yea man, that's cool. I'll watch in a second, but first, just look at this," Joey said, anxious to show Oscar this amazing happening.

"Fine man. Just let me roll this shit up real fast," Oscar said.

"Dude!" Joey screamed. "Put the shit away and look at this!"

Oscar snapped his head towards the computer screen and his mouth and eyes shot wide open.

"What am I lookin at?" asked Oscar, as his eyes wandered over to the number of likes on the page. He scratched his head. "I don't get it. What the hell am I looking at?"

"I made this page about four years ago," said Joey. "I haven't posted a single word on it since then, and it has more than 31 million likes and thousands of messages from people. Hell, man, what if once I start writing things, people tell others, and I get 90 million likes or something? That'd be cool, right?"

"Wait a second. I don't get it. You made a Celebrity Page for 'God' on FaceSpace? And now, out of nowhere, it has thirty-one million likes?" asked Oscar with a very confused look on his face.

Just then Amber came through the door surprising both Joey and Oscar.

"Hey baby!" she said with a bright smile on her face. "I brought you some O-Daisy's. Hope you don't mind some unhealthy fast food tonight. I've been trying to save up some money for a new car. Hey, Oscar. What's up?"

"Normally, I'd say something smart like 'Can you knock?' But I'm in a good mood. Check this out," said Joey.

Amber turned towards his computer.

"Holy shit!" Amber yelled.

"I know. That's what I said!" Joey yelled out, even louder.

"Wow," said a baffled Amber as she saw the large number of likes Joey's page had accumulated. "Here's the crazy thing, guys," said Joey. "It's not even just that people liked it. Check these messages out! It's crazy. I'll click a random one. Read it, babe." Joey said, while holding the down button with his eyes closed to randomize his choice.

Amber read the message dated Feb. 19:

> "Hello God! My name is Andrico Wayans. I just wanted to say thank you for my raise at the Car Wash. My wife and I were having some crazy times and you pulled through just in time. You may have saved my marriage and definitely saved our home. I kept my promise I made to you long ago that if you got me out of this mess that I'd be in church every week. It's been months now and I found your page today. I just wanted to say thank you. I'll remain a faithful Christian. I'll continue to pay my tithes..."

"Let's check out another one. You read this one, Oscar. That way you know I'm not fabricating any of this shit."

Oscar then began to read a message dated Dec. 1st:

> God, you know my name. But I'm not going to

say it out of shame. My sister and I have been feeling things for..."

Oscar panicked and stopped abruptly.

"I'll pick another one....here we go." Dec 28th

"THANK YOU!!!!!! ☺ This is Brian. I'm sixteen years old. I just wanted to tell you that I got the new *Battle Arms: Insane Warfare* game from my grandmother for Christmas! I'm gonna go play it now!!! TIME TO KILL SOME MOTHAFUCKAS!!!"

Joey busted out in laughter. "That's some funny shit. People who love and follow God sure have a funny way of showing their faith. Who writes to *God* and then says 'Time to kill some mothafuckas?'"

Amber then cut in to say, "Well, baby, if everyone were perfect, they wouldn't need Church or God, for that matter, now would they? Don't let this stupid page get to your head, Boo. Don't you have applications to fill out like you said?"

"Yes, baby. But come on. Do you see this?" Joey said, slightly discouraged.

"Of course I see it, baby, and it's pretty...no...VERY cool. But a huge like page for 'God' isn't going to take care of us, and it damn sure ain't going to pay our bills. I had to get O-Daisy's because I'm saving, but I also have to provide for both of us whenever we want to spend time together. I just want it to be like before, baby, when my man could stand on his own two feet. You know how sexy I think that is," said Amber, smiling.

Joey released a huge sigh.

"Yes, baby. Yes, dear. Yes, my love. Yes yes yes! Whatever you want. Whatever you say," Joey said in a mocking tone.

Amber fell into Joey's arms and started to kiss him gently. He responded with a romantic kiss back before she attacked him mid-kiss with a tickle war. Joey started laughing uncontrollably. Amber knew getting tickled was one of his big weaknesses.

Oscar, filming it all on his phone, chuckled and said, "FaceSpace? Definitely someone needs to have some proof that you have a boyfriend, right? I'll tag you in it, Amber."

Amber turned her head to Oscar, still tickling Joey.

"I appreciate that! More effort than he's put in!"

"Thanks, jerk. Not helping!" yelled Joey, while trying to steady his uncontrollable laughter from this tickle torture. "Okay, okay! Get off! I can't take it anymore!"

Amber hopped off of Joey and brushed herself off.

"I hope you learned your lesson, student," said Amber as she smiled. "You better not be a bad boy again or you're getting a spanking next time".

"Yeah? Don't want that now do we?"

"I do!" said Oscar, still filming with his phone and jokingly grabbing onto his manhood.

"You're such a perv," Amber and Joey said together.

They all shared a long laugh, as Joey went back to his computer to log out of his FaceSpace page and look for more jobs to apply for.

Amber grabbed her purse, whipped it over her shoulder, and walked towards Joey's door.

"Okay, Hun, I got to go run home. My mom's been bugging me all day to come have chat with her," said Amber, letting out a hefty groan.

"Okay, but Amber, would you mind quickly writing a resume for me when you get a chance? I'd do it, but I don't have the software. You said it takes like five to ten minutes to make one? Do you mind?"

"No, I don't mind at all," said Amber, slightly annoyed with Joey's constant need for assistance. "I can probably finish that in the next couple days. Text me what you want me to include about your previous work experiences and what not. I think I have all of your other information."

"Thanks!" Joey smiled, knowing that he had just saved himself some more work to do. He turned to Oscar. "So yeah, bro, did you ever grab me that Mountain Mist?"

Oscar formed a frozen and blank stare on his face, looked down at his phone, and then looked back up. "What? No, biatch."

"Fine, I didn't really have the money to pay you back anyway," said Joey, before he turned his back to his computer.

Chapter Six
The Book of Greetings

THE NEXT MORNING, Joey was sleeping when someone banging on his bedroom door woke him up from the snoring coma he had entered. He jumped out of his bed in his boxers and shouted "What! I'm awake!"

"We need to leave for the doctor in fifteen minutes," shouted Joey's mother through the door. "Son, you promised you would bring me today. You know I don't like going to these things by myself!"

Fuckkkk I totally forgot, Joey thought.

"All right!" said Joey. I'll be ready in ten minutes. Just let me brush my teeth." He looked down and noticed his apparent morning wood. "Great, just what I needed," Joey said to himself.

"Make that fifteen minutes! I need to take a quick shower too!" Joey shouted to his mom who had since gone back downstairs to wait for him.

Joey got freshened up and met his mom in the kitchen.

"Hey, Mom, you ready?" he asked, as he went into the fridge to grab a can of Sir Frizz.

"Yes, I'm ready. You know that soda is horrible for you. Have a glass of orange juice or water or something, honey."

"Mom, I'm fine. It's my coffee. You drink coffee, I drink Mountain Mist, but we have none, so it's Sir Frizz. Now let's get you to Doctor Wu's."

Joey and his mom walked out the front door and got into Joey's blue sedan.

"Buckle up, Ma. You know how I drive."

"Yes, like a mad man. Just like your father. Please, son, you know I can't take them crazy turns."

Joey pulled out of his parent's driveway, out onto the road, down the block, and in the direction of the doctor's office a few miles away.

"Son, you know my health isn't too great right now. Please slow down."

"Sorry, Mom," said Joey, as he eased up on the gas pedal

allowing his car to slow from 40 MPH to 25 MPH.

"Thank you, sweetie. So how is that sweet little girlfriend of yours, Amber?"

"She's great, Mom. Hounding me every day about getting a job. Fighting with me every chance she gets."

"Well, just be grateful you have somebody to call your own, dear."

"I am, Mom."

"You know before your father and I met, he had been single for two years. And when we met, he told me I was the love of his life. And within two weeks, he asked me to marry him. Have you even considered marrying this girl, son? You're not getting any younger, and she is just so sweet. And did I mention gorgeous?"

"I just don't know, Mom. Maybe there's somebody else out there for me."

"Yeah, and maybe there's not. Honey, sometimes these chances don't come every day. You may not find somebody as great as her. I'll tell you that right now."

"Okay, Mom. I get it. Thank you for the advice."

Joey turned the volume up on the radio.

They soon arrived at the doctor's office. Joey took his mother's arm and walked her inside to sign in with the receptionist.

"Good afternoon, Mrs. Taylor. How are we doing today?" asked the receptionist whose nametag read *Monica.*

"Oh, I am just dandy, darling. Just here because I want to be!"

"All right, you know the drill. Just put your name on the list, and the doctor will be with you shortly," said Monica.

"Thank you," said Joey, as he signed his mother's name for her and took her to the chairs to wait for her name to be called.

One minute turned into five, which turned into ten as the wait seemed to get longer and longer. Out of boredom, Joey took out his smart phone and decided to download the FaceSpace application that was available for free on any cell phone. The app began to download just as Monica at the front desk called out, "Mrs. Taylor. The doctor is ready to see you."

"Do you want me to come in with you?" asked Joey.

"Nooo, it is all right, sweetie. The fact that you took time out of your busy day to bring me here is enough." His mom laughed and kissed him on the cheek as she got up to head to one of the exam rooms.

"I'll be out here if you need anything, Ma."

Joey looked at his phone as the FaceSpace app completed downloading. He opened it up. It was a tad bit different than the website version, so Joey had to get used to navigating it. Good thing it was an idiot-proof application that anybody could figure out. Joey quickly looked up his page for God and opened it up.

The amount of "likes" he accumulated over the years was still very shocking to him, and he was still trying to digest it. He decided that maybe it was time to write his first post for all of his followers to see.

He clicked on the button that said: "Write Post".

What to say, What to say... Oh I know.

He began typing: Thank you for your patience. I have been here all along and I wan.........."

That's not going to work, he thought, as he quickly erased the whole thing. "All right. Let's try this again," Joey said to himself, trying to sound like a supreme being.

"Thou shalt not ...." Joey began to type, but then he quickly erased those words. He started to type again: "You don't need to believe in me to believe in yourse....." He deleted all that too.

"Ugh. I don't know what to say," Joey yelled aloud, making the other few people in the waiting room look at him like he was nuts.

"Sorry," he said to them, as they went back to minding their own business.

After a few more attempts at writing the perfect first post, he was about to give up. But then he decided to type what he considered might be the most almighty thought he could think of for his first post.

"Hi," was all he put. It was published at 11:23 A.M on August 10th.

Ahhhh, that sounds better, Joey thought.

He then exited the FaceSpace app and quietly waited for his mother to come back to the waiting room. He looked up a few videos on ViewTube to pass the time.

After about 45 minutes, his mother returned, and Joey drove her home.

He parked his car in the driveway and turned off the engine.

"Hold on, Mom," said Joey as he got out of his car, running to the other side to open up the door for his mother. He reached down to help her out of the seat.

"Thank you, son," said his mother, getting out of his car. "You really are a sweetheart. I'm glad I raised such a wonderful young man. I hope you find what you are looking for, Joseph."

"I love you, Mom," he said before running up to his room and jumping into bed, where he was going to attempt to go back to sleep.

His phone vibrated just he slid under his messy comforter and into his three cushy pillows. He took out his phone and saw it was Amber. He decided to ignore it and threw it onto his bedside table.

Within in seconds, Joey had crashed into his warmed cozy abyss of a nap. As he began to drift off into dreams that involved God, Amber, and lord knows what else, he began to snore loudly for the first time in a long while.

He woke up a few hours later, around 5:35, to the smell of his favorite Italian meal being cooked downstairs. He opened his eyes and took in the aroma that smelled like chicken parmesan. As he hopped out of bed, he threw on the shirt he was wearing before, grabbed his cell phone, and hobbled on downstairs to join his family.

His father was finishing up cooking dinner as his mother was setting the table.

"So nice of you to join us, son," said Joey's father.

"Ahhh, suck it, Pops," Joey replied as he walked down the stairs.

"Watch your language, Joseph," said his mother, as she continued setting the table with silverware and napkins.

"It's okay, Frannie. He wants me to suck it because Amber hasn't sucked his in months," said his father, cracking up.

"Watch your mouth too. That is disgusting," said Joey's mother.

"Very funny, Dad."

"Can you go get your sister from her room and tell her dinner is ready," his father asked.

"Yeah, whatever," said Joey, as he darted up the stairs two at a time.

He arrived at his sister Jane's room and banged on the door. "Hey! Dinner's ready, fucker!" he yelled to his sister.

"I'll be right out, fuck face!" Joey's eighth grade sister yelled back.

Joey's family sat down together to eat dinner like they did most nights of the week, with the exceptions of a couple days when Joey's father worked late and they all just ate in their rooms.

The food smelled amazing as Joey began to dig in to the perfectly-breaded chicken cutlets, smothered in real, homemade tomato sauce and mozzarella mixed with melted parmesan cheese on top of a bed of thin spaghetti.

Joey's mother smacked his hands away from the plates of food and said, "No! We say grace in this house. No exceptions."

"Ughhhhhh. Alright. Alright," said Joey.

"Jane, dear, won't you please do the honors?" asked their father.

The family all held hands around the table, as Joey's sister Jane began to say grace.

"Thank you, God, for this amazing food we are about to eat. Thank you for watching over my family and me. For helping my older brother, who can sometimes be a jackass, find a job."

"Hey," said Joey.

"Oh, calm down," Jane said. "Sorry. Please forgive my brother for rudely interrupting, and, most of all, look over my mother and her health and help her get better for all of us. Amen."

"Amen!" said everyone else at the table.

Then they all dug into the food. Joey's dad broke off pieces of garlic bread for everybody as he tried to serve his wife and kids a healthy dose of salad. He also had homemade eggplant parmesan, specifically for his wife who had become a vegetarian because of the heart problems she discovered over the last few years.

"Everything looks amazing, Jim," said Joey's mother.

"Thank you, Babe."

The family all ate, silently, as they kept to themselves before Joey's father spoke.

"Soooo, Jane, you have a big test coming up next week. Have you been studying?"

"Yes, Dad. You know I am. Why are you even asking me? Maybe you should ask Joey if he got a job this week? He's the only 26 year old I know who still lives at home with his parents."

"Shut up, asshole," said Joey.

"Bite me," Jane said.

"Want me to tell Mom and Dad about how you were touching your boyfriend's dick when I walked in on you the other day?"

"What the hell, Jane!" shouted her father.

"You dickhead!" Jane yelled at Joey.

"Don't mess with me, sis," Joey replied, as he continued to eat his tasty Italian dinner.

As his parents started to question their daughter, Joey tuned them all out, wondering if anyone had responded to his first FaceSpace post as "God." He put down his fork and opened up the FaceSpace app on his smart phone and entered his password, as it booted up to the front page. He found his God page and clicked on it. When it opened up, there was a sign of 10,000+ notifications. Joey had no idea what that meant, being unfamiliar with the social network site. He clicked on the icon and it appeared that Joey had 12,320 Likes and 5,906 Comments on the initial post he made earlier.

Joey pushed his chair back from the table. "Holy fuckin shit."

"Hey!!! Watch your mouth," said Joey's mother.

Joey looked up from his cell phone screen.

"Did I say that out loud? Sorry."

"What it is?"

"Ah...Nothing, Mom. Oscar just sent me a new movie trailer for this flick we've both been dying to see."

"Must be one heck of a movie. You gave me a shock."

"Yeah, don't scare your mother," said his father.

"I'm sorry," said Joey as he looked down and clicked on the comments.

One read: "We knew you would be back!" Another one said: "Our savior is here!"

A third wrote "Hello! From Hong Kong!"

There were thousands more.

Joey stood up from the table. "I'm finished. Dinner was really good. Thanks for the chow, guys."

He brought his plate to the kitchen and cleaned off his dish putting his plate into the sink.

"You're still an asshole!" Jane screamed out.

Joey returned to the table, kissed his mother on the cheek, and walked out, flipping his middle finger to his sister, which resulted in her flipping one right back.

He laughed as he looked down at his phone and rushed upstairs to his room.

He texted his friend Oscar:

> Dude, go check my God page on FaceSpace! Shit is about to go down!

Joey grabbed his dirty socks and tossed them into the pile of laundry.

Chapter Seven
The Book of Society

OSCAR TEXTED JOEY.

> Dude, what the shit? You're like a celebrity

Joey texted back.

> That's sort of how it feels man. What's something harmless I could post?

> I dunno man. I never once even thought of having over like 700 friends, let alone over 31 million followers. I'd tell everyone to jump off a bridge or something. LOL

Joey texted.

> You're such an asshole. I thought I was bad

> You *are* bad. I was just joking. Your the type of guy that would do it for real because you *h8 ppl*

> Not true. And it's 'you're' not 'your.' Did you even graduate the fourth grade? Hey. I'm getting texted from Amber."

Joey's phone vibrated as Amber's text arrived:

> Baby, I'm almost done. I just need to go back and edit your work history.

Joey ignored Amber and opened up Oscar's conversation and coincidentally Oscar's bubble popped up:

> You're, your, whatever. Maybe you can tell every one of YOUR followers to do something or whatever. See what happens.

Joey sat for a moment and thought to himself, *Hmm.* He shrugged his shoulders then ran downstairs.

"Do you and Mom have a FaceSpace account," he asked his dad.

"What the hell is that?"

*Two people I thought would have it...*Joey thought.

"You guys should get one," he said. "It's a good way to connect to people. Your siblings probably have one, I'm sure. I'm sure Uncle Petey has one, that crazy bastard."

His dad pondered a bit. "Maybe I could use a way to get in touch with our family and what not."

"Exactly..."

"Wait a second. I thought you were against that social media crap. Didn't you go on a tantrum and delete your MyFace profile a few years ago?" asked his dad.

"Yeah. But FaceSpace is sort of like the new and improved MyFace."

"Maybe I will make an account," said Joey's dad. "Why not? I can't even find my buddy George I knew back in high school. Maybe he's on that website or something."

"Maybe, Dad."

If I'm going to do this, I may as well have some fun with it, Joey thought, as he grabbed himself another Sir Frizz from the fridge. He headed back upstairs to his room and turned on some music through his Wizard's Box app that played songs from different groups based on your taste in music.

He picked up a *Rubik's* cube that he'd been working on for a few weeks now to pass the time. After a solid two minutes, he grew bored with it as his mind returned to his new-found enjoyment. *Gotta find something to do until I know the perfect thing to write on FaceLame,* Joey thought.

He couldn't help but get on his FaceSpace. He navigated around and saw the 'Games' tab on the left side of the screen. Feeling like a hypocrite, being that he was in his own little world at the moment, void of reality, he clicked it on to secure a sense of integrity.

He saw a bunch of different games, all seeming to be low graphic puzzles.

Wow, these games look hilarious.

Joey began scrolling down to check out different games and what they were about. They all had very vague descriptions. "Veggie Smash"— Match vegetables and earn points! "Ruby Drop" — Drop rubies onto small lizards. Watch out. If you fail, they'll chuckle and trust! You'll be infuriated! "Larry Jotter"— a game/app where you draw a picture and send it to others, they then draw another piece of the picture and eventually it makes a full picture that gets sent to everyone involved in the drawing.

"Save the Princess" — You run around as a small-scale carpenter that is on a quest to save a princess named Tulip from the evil Vampire Xandler.

"POP: Pissed Off Penguins" — You shoot penguins out of a cannon as they try to smash into a bunch of chickens as they're in a war for flying bird supremacy.

All of them had a version you could pay for and a version that was free, but you had to deal with a lot of advertisements when you used the free versions. Joey had expressed his hatred for ads many times before. The list went on and on and on as Joey began skimming faster and faster.

These are so dumb looking, he thought, as he finally closed out the screen. *I can't believe people paid three bucks for that shit.*

Joey turned on his TV and set up his old streamer box so he could watch Internet content on his television. He opened up the DotFilmz app that allowed you to watch a variety of movies, TV shows, documentaries, etc., whenever you want. He put on a movie named *A Day Scream on Weary Lane,* a classic horror movie from his childhood. After not quite ten minutes, he began wondering what he could do on his FaceSpace page. After about an hour of wondering, he drifted off.

Joey awoke at 2:58 a.m., remembering one particular dream: A sea of people were following him. He was walking through a crazy world of knives, fire, and his darkest fears, including sharks and explosions. They were all floating around in a limitless space that surrounded him, almost suffocating him. But his people behind him kept him strong. He was wearing a red T-Shirt and all of his followers were wearing white T-Shirts.

He jumped out of bed seeing the big green block on the screen asking if he'd like to watch the next movie in the queue. He grabbed his phone and sent a mass text to Oscar, Amber, Chris, Tyson, Cody, and Henry:

> Guys! When you wake up go on FaceSpace and like the God page if you haven't already, and then check to see what it says.

He immediately received a text message back from Tyson that read:

> Dude, I'm literally texting you back while gettin' sum head right now!

Instantaneously Joey got another message from Tyson, a picture of him and Oscar's aunt sharing an intimate moment with her trying, too late, to cover her face. Joey felt like he was going to throw up, nauseated by the picture message.

A few seconds later, he got a text from Oscar.

> I'm already awake man. I can't fall asleep. My aunt and her boyfriend are upstairs fucking harder and louder than EVER b4. It's bordering on the point of ridiculous at this point.

Joey laughed, knowing the truth and all. Everyone else must have been sleeping, as he didn't get any more texts by the time he splashed water on his face.

He then sat down at his computer, trying to believe in himself as a powerful being. He assumed a perfect posture, brought his fingers to the keyboard, and typed:

> In honor of me and the symbol of purity, wear a white T-Shirt today.

His message was posted at 3:00 AM on August 11th.

Joey, since he was still wide awake at three in the morning, decided to try something to help him drift back to sleep. He resumed playing *A Day Scream on Weary Lane* from the position it paused when he last fell asleep. The movie finished after about forty minutes, but Joey was still wide awake.

Oy, everyone's asleep. No one to text. Joey looked around his room for something to do. His Wizard's Box was calling his name as the silence in his room drove him mad.

He cut the volume down to make sure he didn't wake anyone in the house and sat at his computer. He refused to look at the God post because he believed it was too soon. He knew that when he did look at it, he'd be in awe again. He wanted to wait until it grew a bit. Little did he know it had already received eight thousand likes, just shy of twelve thousand comments, and seven thousand shares. To waste more time, he went back to the games and clicked on POP: Pissed Off Penguins. Joey started blasting them out of cannons.

Wow, this is actually quite challenging for some 16-bit looking game.

Joey had seen most of the newer games that look closer to real life than life itself. Something so primitive shouldn't be so hard.

Losing track of time, he continued to shoot penguins out of the cannons and at the chickens. At 3:58, he got to level three. At 4:24, he got to level six, and at 6:32, he found himself on level twenty. *Man, this is pretty addicting. I see why people get into these things. Maybe they're not so bad.* Joey thought, as he enjoyed the game.

Eight a.m. crept in, and Joey began to feel like taking a short nap. He played the level he was stuck on a couple of more times until he eventually gave up after a few good yawns and headed to his bed. He lay on top of the covers and rested his eyes.

When Joey woke back up it was 11:09 a.m. *Man...I'm hungry as shit.* He slid out of bed, grabbed his phone, and headed to the kitchen. He preheated the oven and headed to the bathroom where he sat on the toilet and checked his messages.

Amber was the only one with an unread message icon. Joey opened it up and read:

> "Wow dear. You never sent me your work history, but you can write me at 3a.m. about some stupid FaceSpace page. Look, we really need to have a talk. I'll see you later tonight or tomorrow."

Joey closed the text, washed his hands, and then left the bathroom. He headed back into the kitchen and threw a bagel into the oven.

Going back to his phone, which was slowly becoming his biggest source of entertainment, FaceSpace included, he opened up Pissed Off Penguins again, determined to pass level twenty. After a few minutes, he still hadn't beaten it. So he decided he'd try another game. Joey tried his luck with Ruby Drop. After a few lizards got bonked by a few rubies and four levels later, Joey smelled something burning.

"Who's burning food!?" his mother screamed.

"Sorry, Mom," said Joey. "I got it." He scrambled to grab some mittens to get the pan holding the bagel out of the stove. He spread some cream cheese over his burned bagel and woofed it down before heading back upstairs to pick out the clothes he'd be wearing to the mall.

Joey jumped in the shower, FaceSpace and its world still fresh on his mind. *I wonder if people really pay for those games. The only difference is an ad.*

Fast-forward ten minutes, and Joey was on his way to the mall. About halfway there, he noticed his gas tank was getting closer to 'E' than he would like. He quickly schemed together what seemed like a good plan and texted Tyson.

> Sorry bro but I'm desperate. I need to borrow ten bucks to throw in my gas tank or I'm telling Oscar and Erica's BF about your little time together.

Minutes later, Tyson sent a text back:

> Aww, that's fucked up! All right man. In an hour or so, check your mailbox. I'll have it in there for ya

> Thanks man, and I'm sorry LOL

Joey texted back.

> No problem bro. Times are
> hard. I understand

Joey looked up to find he was well over the yellow line on the road and swerved back. Luckily for him, the road was pretty clear. He stopped at a traffic light and thought about the weird dream he had. Thirty seconds felt like two, as the light turned green again, only to hear a honk behind him to tell him so. As he sped off to the mall, his phone alerted him twice that his FaceSpace God page had two new followers - his parents, Jim and Fran Taylor.

Joey let out a big laugh.

He pulled up at the mall and noticed something strange. He couldn't really put his finger on it, but he knew something was rather odd. It became more obvious when he entered the mall and saw a large number of people wearing white T-shirts. He quickly counted only twenty people that didn't have on a white T-shirt.

Joey froze at the entrance. He tried to walk forward at a normal pace, but could barely move. He quickly lost control and had a huge outburst of laughter. Everyone stared at him, as if he was nuts. Feeling embarrassed, he snapped back into reality and apologized to everyone around him. He then pressed the video camera option on his phone. He looked around at all of the white shirts the people in the shopping mall were wearing. He started recording the sea of white that surrounded him. He did this all the way to the CompuNerd store where he had a gift certificate with a remaining balance of $401.23.

Joey bought a new anti-virus program for his PC that was on sale for 75% off. He looked around the store for a possible future purchase. He saw a bunch of FaceSpace currency cards that sold for $3, $5, $10, and $20, all of which gave you about twenty times the amount in FaceSpace money than real money. He also noticed that they were carrying the newer version of the *Battle Arms: Insane Warfare* game that was mentioned in the e-mail that the sixteen-year-old kid, Brian, had written to God in December. There was also an ad for the next game, *Battle Arms: Chemical Warfare*.

Joey was about to note that as a possible future buy when his cell phone went off. He struggled to get it off of his waist clip holster and checked his text.

Henry wrote him:

> Hey dude! So I just got a chance to watch 'This Will Scare You' and yes, it scared me! LOL. I'm gonna run by and borrow another if I can

Joey texted back:

> You can man, but you should really just start using my DotFlimz account. It'd be hell of a lot easier

He looked at a few more things in the store before going to the counter to pay for his items. The girl that works there—her nametag read *Courchesny*—greeted Joey with a big smile

"Hey!," said Courchesny. "I see you around here a lot. This is my first time on the register though. How are you?"

He was about to respond when his phone interrupted with another text from Henry. It read:

> I would bro, but our wireless has been fucking up lately. I'll bring back the other three I owe you too. I keep forgetting

Joey skimmed through the message but didn't answer back, as he didn't want to be rude to the checkout girl ringing up his items. He put the phone back onto his holster all his friends made fun of him for having.

"I'm doin' great," said Joey. "Thanks for asking."

Joey gave Courchesny the once-over. He was especially attracted to her cheekbones for whatever reason and her large smile helped too.

She put the items in a bag. "That'll be $11.32 after taxes. Would you like to add some FaceSpace credits for as low as $3? It'll give you $60 to spend on the site for games, advertising, and stuff."

Not wanting to seem like a cheap guy, Joey accepted the offer.

She charged him the extra $3 and bid him farewell.

"Thank you very much," said Joey, as he made his way back towards the entrance of the mall, continuing to film and snap pictures in complete astonishment at the absolute sea of people wearing their white T-shirts. He stopped at the entrance again, took one more scan around the area with his phone, and headed back to his FaceSpace page to check on his status.

To his complete surprise, his follower count now read 42.9 million, and his T-shirt status post had already hit 20,017 likes, 54,043 comments, and 18,075 shares.

Oh...my.... me? Joey though, as he headed back to his car, passing by hundreds of people that must have seen his post on FaceSpace because they were wearing white T-shirts.

Chapter Eight
The Book of Freedom

THAT FRIDAY NIGHT, Joey and Amber went out to dinner and the movies. They had Mexican food at Joey's favorite restaurant, Faber's Fajitas, and argued throughout the entire meal. Joey ended up paying for the meal with his nearly maxed-out credit card as they rushed out in time to make the 9 p.m. movie they had planned on seeing all week. It was a romantic comedy Amber had been begging Joey to take her to, *Broken Roses*.

They arrived at the movie theater ten minutes late, but because of previews, they were walking in just as the opening credits to the movie started.

The movie lasted two hours and fifteen minutes, but to Joey it felt like a lifetime. He dozed off a few times before his girlfriend woke him up with a nudge. It was not his cup of tea when it came to films. But he was trying to please her. He felt a difference in her mood and attitude towards him as of late and wasn't exactly sure what he had done wrong.

They drove back to Amber's apartment, which she shared with her best friend, Stephanie. Joey drove in silence, trying to grab Amber's hand, but she was a little hesitant. She was acting somewhat strange compared to what he was used to.

"What's wrong, babe," asked Joey? "Nothing."

"Well, did you like the movie at least?" He tried to rub her leg to comfort her, but she pulled out her phone and texted one of her friends.

"Hmmmmm, all right. What did I do?" Joey asked,

"It's nothing. The movie was great. You may have known that if you didn't keep falling asleep every five minutes."

"I fell asleep twice, if I remember correctly. I'm sorry, but it was just a little bit boring."

Joey slowed the car down and stopped at a red light.

"It was more than two times, Joseph. But that's not why I'm mad, okay?"

"Please share with the class, babe. Because we would all love to know what's wrong."

Joey kept trying to put his hand on her leg, but she kept smacking it off.

"Wow, I see how it is," said Joey, as he stopped trying.

"Look, Joseph. I don't know how to say this. Tonight was a great attempt, and it was sweet you wanted to take me out on a date. But I have been thinking about a lot of things lately."

Uh oh, this can't be good, Joey thought, as he turned down the street of Amber's apartment.

"What have you been thinking about, babe?" Joey asked, as he took in a big gulp.

"Joey, you haven't had a job in three months. I know it's not all about that, but I have been trying to help you with your resume, and you have been no help at all. How am I going to help you get a job if you can't even give me what I need to help you, huh?"

"I'm trying, Amber." Joey said.

"Well, obviously not hard enough." said Amber.

"That's fucked up, babe."

"That's tough love, Joseph."

"Look, I'm going to get a job any day now. One of these places is going to call me and I'll be back to normal, okay," said Joey as he pulled into the parking lot of Amber's apartment complex. He found an empty parking spot, and started to pull into it.

"That's reserved parking only," said Amber.

"I don't care. Who the hell is going to say something?" Joey turned the key in the ignition and shut off his car.

"Whatever. You always have to get your way," she said, getting out of the car.

"Baby, calm down."

Joey got out as well and then grabbed Amber by the waist and pulled her closer to him next to his car in the parking lot.

"Joseph!" she cried out, as she was literally swept off her feet and lifted off the ground as Joey started to kiss her on the lips leading down to her neck.

"Joey, you know that's my weak spoooooo..." Amber was cut off as Joey started to lick her neck and suck on it in a circular motion using just the right amount of tongue. She couldn't help but give in and started to kiss him back, rubbing his stomach, putting her hands lower and lower on his body as the two made out. Neighbors looked out their window—one in particular shut their blinds because they were trying to sleep, considering it was already almost midnight.

"All right. You convinced me," said Amber. "Let's get upstairs. But you can't sleep over. I have a lot to do tomorrow and the rest of the weekend."

"That's fine."

Joey took her hand and followed Amber down the walkway to her apartment. They had to take the steps to the second floor which was where Amber's place was.

She stuck the key in the lock and opened the door, pulling Joey in behind her.

He pushed her up against the door they had just closed behind them and Amber wrapped her legs around him, as he kissed her, feeling her body from up to down.

"Oh, I like that, baby."

Joey reached beneath her shirt and began to unhook her bra. He pulled it out through the neck of her shirt, and it turned her on even more.

"Look at you, go," she said. "Where'd you learn that?" Amber asked, as he started to feel her breasts through her shirt.

"I got a lot of tricks up my sleeve you don't know about."

Joey continued to make her go crazy with sensation. He went back to kissing her neck, and pulled her towards the kitchen counter and started dry humping her body.

Amber let out a loud moan, as he moved his hand down her legs. The moan was so loud it could probably wake up some of the neighbors. Just then Amber's roommate walked out of her bedroom, carrying a baseball bat. She immediately noticed Amber and Joey getting hot and heavy in the kitchen, stopped in her tracks, and turned around towards her room.

"Sorry to interrupt," said her roommate, as she vanished back into her dark room, where you could hear gangsta rap music rumbling through the walls.

Joey and Amber took the party to her room, where they embraced each other like it was their first time making love. They had steamy, passionate sex for about an hour. Amber yelled out loud that Joey made her "go" multiple times, and he finally got off around an hour into their lovemaking. It may have been the best sex they had ever had, especially in Joey's eyes.

"That was amazing," said Amber, as she lay in her bed with her legs spread wide without a care in the world. They were both sweating profusely as Joey hopped up to go into the bathroom and clean up.

When Joey returned to Amber's bedroom, they got dressed. Joey gathered his things, and Amber walked him out to his car.

"I hope you had fun tonight," said Joey, as they walked down the walkway to the parking lot.

"I did, for the most part. Thanks for taking me out on a nice date."

They drew closer to Joey's car.

"All right. Good. I'm glad."

Joey squeezed her hand. Amber gently squeezed it back, then pulled away.

"Listen, Joe."

"I know. I'm sorry for falling asleep in the movie earlier. You know I didn't mean to."

"It's not that, Joseph. I need to tell you something."

"I love you too, babe!"

Joey went in to kiss his girlfriend, who ducked away.

"I...I...I think we need to break up."

Joey's cute smile turned into a frown.

"What?"

"I just think we are in two totally different places in our life. I am just starting my career. You have a few kinks to work out. I don't think we should be together right now."

"Babe, I promise you. I am trying to find a job. I'm not just sitting around doing nothing you know."

As he said those words he thought, *that's exactly what I'm doing.*

"Look, Joseph. It's not you, it's me."

"Bullshit! That's the most clichéd line you could feed me, Amber."

"I'm sorry. I hope everything works out for you."

"This isn't fair! I didn't do anything to deserve this. Throughout our relationship, all of the women I've turned down. I never cheated on you once. This is fucked up. I can't believe you."

"You will be just fine."

"No. Fuck this. I can't believe you're doing this to me!"

Joey felt himself about to tear up a bit. He never cried, but he couldn't stop the water from leaving his eyes.

"Well, you can't act like you didn't see this coming."

"You just took me upstairs and had sex with me! What the fuck was that about? You could have just told me earlier."

Joey wiped a tear from his face.

"You turned me on. I couldn't stop myself. Plus, I thought you deserved one more time with me."

"This is fucked up. You're an asshole for this."

"I know you're just upset right now, so I won't take that comment seriously," said Amber.

Joey thought about how the whole world was crashing around him. But for some reason, he stopped crying and became numb. He had suddenly lost all care for her and he started heading toward his car.

"You're going to be sorry you broke this off. I promise you that," Joey said.

He opened the door to his blue sedan.

"Maybe, someday, but right now I can't do it. I can't do 'us.'"

"I'm going to change the world. I'm going to make a shit load of money, and you're gonna feel so stupid you left me."

"Oh yeah? How the hell is that? You gonna ask your new found followers for money?"

Joey stopped and thought, *That's actually not a bad idea.*

"Bye, bitch."

Joey flipped her off, hopped into his car, started it up, and sped out of the parking lot like the building was about to explode in flames.

As soon as Joey arrived back at his house, he immediately ran upstairs to his room. He thought, *Stupid thot is going to be sorry.*

He sat down at his computer desk, logged on to FaceSpace, and clicked on his God page. He thought long and hard about what he wanted to say. He also thought about how his girlfriend just broke up with him. Joey couldn't stop thinking about how broke he was, and that his puny unemployment checks were going to stop coming any day now.

His thoughts turned to Amber again, and he started to get really upset. *I'll show her.* He remembered the company she worked for, an app called AllTalk and how it was launching a large social networking campaign. His first thought was to sabotage it.

Joey clicked on the 'Write Post' button and began to type.

> To all of my beloved followers,
>
> You may or may not have heard of the app, AllTalk. I want to warn you all, this is an evil company. A disgusting corporation full of greed. The people who run this company are known racists. And they trick you into downloading their app. Then they make you automatically pay for it by sending you charges at ridiculous rates through your cell phone service so you aren't even aware of it.
>
> BOYCOTT ALLTALK!
>
> If you already have this app, please delete it if you know what's best for you!
>
> Also, if you would, leave very bad reviews and comments on the download page for the app. We need to take these people down before they steal more of my people's money!
>
> Thanks for listening,
> Bless You All,
> God

Joey clicked *publish post*, and the message went out to his forty two million followers all around the world through FaceSpace. Almost immediately after hitting the *publish post* button, he felt a little bad about defaming the company; they hadn't done anything specifically wrong to him, except for the fact that his now ex-girlfriend Amber worked there.

Joey went to the bathroom, and by the time he got back to his computer, he saw the post was already being shared, liked, and commented on by thousands and thousands more of his followers by the second.

I told you you'd be sorry. Joey started laughing. "I hate bitches," he said to himself.

Chapter Nine
The Book of Revolution

JOEY CLICKED ON THE *Write Post* button and began to type: *Even God Has Feelings*

Even God Feels Alone

He then clicked *Publish* before spinning from his chair and running downstairs. He walked into the kitchen and opened up the refrigerator.

Joey looked around at the random food his parents had. None of it looked too appetizing, so he grabbed a few cold cuts from the bottom container — ham, turkey, and provolone cheese. He reached into the cabinet and grabbed some fresh white bread, then pulled out some mayonnaise and mustard and proceeded to make a couple of sandwiches.

Joey grabbed a handful of pretzels from the pantry and piled them onto a paper plate accompanied by the two turkey and ham sandwiches. He went back into the refrigerator and pulled out some orange juice. Then he grabbed a cup out of the cupboard and poured himself a glass. He then went back up to his room.

Joey logged back onto his FaceSpace page for God and scrolled down to see the post he made the day before about the AllTalk Corporation.

He was surprised to see there were 40,013 plus likes and it was shared over 60,029 times as well. He then scrolled down below to read the comments.

One writer commented early that morning at 3:43 a.m.

> All right Lord. We Will Do As You Please. Just deleted the app, left a bad review and even sent an email to the company. These people must be stopped.

"Wow," Joey said to himself, as he realized his plan was working just as he thought it would.

Another wrote:

> Amen, Every1 boycott AllTalk Now!!

Another comment read:

I will be spreading this message. Thank You God for the heads up.

Joey couldn't stop reading; he read 30 comments before he had to take a break. *This is crazy.*

A large bang on Joey's bedroom door scared him as he screamed out, "What?"

"It's me," yelled Jane, "Let me in, you brat!"

"Okay. Hold on!"

Joey got up from his chair, walked over, unlocked his door, and opened it up for his sister.

"What do you want?"

She barged in and sat down on his bed.

"Nothing, you jerk. I just wanted to ask if you would give me and my friends a ride to the movies tonight. Mom said she wouldn't take us."

"I don't know, Jane. I have a lot to do tonight, and you shouldn't be going out on a Saturday night. You're only in middle school. If Mom said 'no' then I'm not getting in the middle of it."

Joey sat back down on his spinning chair.

"C'monnnnnn, broooo."

"Naaaaa."

He continued to troll his followers.

"Please. I'll owe you one!"

"Uh huh."

"What is that you got there? I thought you were against FaceSpace or something?"

"Ohhh...Uhhhhh...I don't know," Joey said, as he kept scrolling up and down his page.

"No, really. I thought you deleted your page like forever ago. Weren't you like against all social networking, if I remember correctly?"

"Yeah, I was," said Joey. "But something happened..."

"Oh yeah? What's that?" asked his sister.

"Well. It's kind of a long story. But to make it short, I made this celebrity page for God, like four years ago. I forgot it existed for the most part when I decided to get off the grid. Recently, I remembered that I made the page, and brought it up to Amber. Before we broke up, she told me I should see if it's still out there somewhere. I found it, and to my surprise, it had over 30 million likes. I couldn't believe it. At first, I wasn't going to post anything on it, but I decided to say 'Fuck It' and brought it back to life. As soon as I made my first post, people have been liking, commenting, and sharing my posts like crazy."

Joey went on before his sister interrupted him. "I really can't believe the reaction I'm getting. I've gotten ten million more likes in the last week. It's crazy. My God page has almost 43 million likes now. I never realized how much impact the Internet could have on so many millions of people. It's really unreal."

"Wait a second. You and Amber broke up?"

"Yeah. She broke up with me last night. But that's not the point."

"So, wow. That's pretty cool, big bro. I didn't know you had it in you, really."

"Why's that?" asked Joey.

"Well, you've always been sort of an anti-social person. I didn't think you would ever take to social media, for anything," said Jane.

"Yeah, well. I didn't really care about keeping up with people. If they knew me, they had my number. I don't need to update people every day with what I ate for lunch, or who I am dating lately."

"Yeah, I've heard you say that before."

"I mean really. Who really cares what the hell you had for dinner? Stop taking pictures of your damned meal and just enjoy it. Damn."

"Yeah, yeah, yeah."

"Whatever."

His sister just stared at her brother, amazed at this change in him, as Joey went onto Findoo to research something new he was thinking about posting. But he became distracted by an article entitled "18 Celebrities you didn't know were bi-sexual."

"Wow, so you said you have forty million likes on this page?"

"Yeah, probably more like forty-three or even forty-five million by today. I am getting a million or two more every day. I forgot what number it's up to by now."

"Sooooo, you know you want to post my most recent cover of Emily Biggins' new single 'Carry Me.' It did really good. I just need it to get that bump, so more people can see it, you know."

Joey started to laugh out loud. "You're kidding me, right, Lil Sis? I'm sorry, but I won't sell out my page to anybody, and that includes my baby sister. I'm sorry."

"Okay, fine, whatever. I didn't think you would anyway. But I just want to say, I'm sorry Amber broke up with you. She was a bitch anyway. I never liked her. You deserve much better, Joe."

He looked over at his sister and, for the first time in a while, he was really happy with her for calling someone a bitch.

"You know, how about you call your friend and tell her I'll bring you guys to the movies?"

"Thank you so much, Joey. You're the best."

Jane stood up and hugged her brother for the first time in a long time with a genuine smile she could not fake even if she had tried.

"All right. You owe me one."

"I'll be ready to go in about an hour," said Jane, as she left Joey's room.

Joey felt his pants vibrating before he pulled out his phone and saw it was Oscar calling him. He put his phone to his ear, as he pushed back on his spinning chair, rolling across his floor to his closet.

"Hey man," said Oscar.

"What's going on, Oscar?"

"I was wondering. Doesn't your girlfriend work for that company AllTalk?"

"She's not my girlfriend anymore. But yeah, Amber works there. Why, what's up?" asked Joey.

"Wait. You guys broke up? When did that happen bro? You all right?"

"Yeah, man. I'm tryna get over it. I hate her."

"I'm sorry, bro. Girls can be whack sometimes," said Oscar.

"Yeah."

"So what else you up to?" asked Oscar.

"Wait. What were you going to say about AllTalk?" Joey asked excitingly.

"Oh yeah. I just saw an article online about it —something about how the owners are racist and a bunch of other crap. I was worried Amber was at risk in losing her new job. Reporters were saying they expect to see the stock of the new app company drop any day this week," Oscar explained.

"Wow. That's absolutely nuts," Joey responded.

"Yeah, I thought so. But if y'all broke up then fuck her, right?"

"Oh, yeah. Definitely fuck her," Joey agreed.

"Anyway, what you doin' later?" asked Oscar.

"Gotta bring my sister to the movies. Then just hanging out. How about you?"

"Nothing really. You wanna get up and do something?"

"Yeah. If you want to come over to my parent's house, we can hang out or something," said Joey.

"Sure, man," said Oscar. "I'll be over in an hour or two."

"Make it an hour, man, okay?"

"Sounds good." Oscar went on.

"Want to drink, man? Sounds like you can use a drink."

"Naaaa. You know I don't drink like that."

"Whatever. I'm still drinking. I'll see you in a little bit man."

Joey hung up on Oscar and pulled up Findoo on his cell phone to look up the recent news about AllTalk. He was freaking out, thinking about what could happen to Amber. Then he remembered that he was still mad at her.

He read an article that included the following:

> This just in... All over folks are taking to the Internet to express their concern and distress towards upcoming startup app, AllTalk. The two co-owners, Jack Willow and Paul Smith, are said to be racist and at one time said they don't want minorities using their product. There was no proof of them saying this, but a source close to the company leaked the information.
>
> Many people have posted blogs against the app, leaving distasteful reviews on the app, all over FaceSpace, and sending very hateful messages to the company..."

Joey clicked out of the article, and went back to his FaceSpace page to think of the next post he was going to make as their new leader.

Do I really have this much power?

He went to the top of the page and clicked on *Write Post*.

Joey then typed: If you had the chance to change the world in one way, how would you change it?

He clicked *Publish Post* before he sat back to watch the answers unfold. He then heard a knock on his door.

"Hey, Joe. I'm ready to leave whenever you are," said his sister from the other side of his bedroom door.

"Okay. I'll be out in five minutes."

Joey started to see the comments pile up from the question he just asked his followers as he shut down his computer, threw on his sweatshirt, and walked out his room. He immediately saw Jane dressed up a tad different than what he was used to seeing her in.

"Wow. Look at you, good ol' Tom Boy in the flesh."

"Shut the hell up!"

Jane punched her brother in the arm.

"That doesn't hurt," said Joey, as he started to walk out the front door of their house.

"Sshhhhh," said Jane. "I don't want Mom and Dad to hear us."

"You mean you don't want Mom and Dad to see you leaving!"

They hopped into Joey's car, and he sped out of their driveway.

"Do you remember how to get to Julia's house? She and Katherine are waiting there for us."

"Yeah, she lives off of Old Grove Lane, if I remember correctly," said Joey.

"Yep, right next to that creepy blue house," Jane said.

Joey and his sister picked up her friends who were all in her class in middle school. He drove them to the mall that had the LMC8 movie theatre with large 3D screens.

He pulled up to the box office to let his sister and her friends out.

"You guys be safe. Don't get into any trouble," said Joey as the girls hopped out of the back seat.

"Thanks, big bro," said Jane. "Like I said, I owe you one".

"Do y'all have a ride home?"

"I'm not sure. Can I text you in an hour or two if I need one?"

"Damn. I'm going to be hanging out with Oscar. But yeah, I suppose so. I don't want you guys stranded out here. I have no clue what kinds of people lurk around here at midnight."

"All right. Thanks Joe."

Jane and her friends ran to the box office to purchase tickets. Joey drove back home to meet up with his best friend. Oscar was sitting on the trunk of his green cruiser when Joey pulled into his driveway.

"What's upppp?" asked Oscar as Joey put his car into park before turning it off.

"Not much, my man. This FaceSpace stuff is just getting really crazy."

Joey gave Oscar a high five.

Oscar had a brown bag next to him containing a large bottle of whiskey.

"So...I know you don't drink, like ever. But maybe you may want to grow some hair on your chest and balls tonight and drink some of this bottle with me."

Oscar held the bottle up with a big smirk on his face.

"Motherrr fuckerrrrr," said Joey, as he started to have flashbacks to the last time he ended up drinking with Oscar and he woke up in a puddle of his own vomit the next day.

"Ehhhhhh, I don't know, man. Probably not tonight."

"Don't be a pussy bro!" said Oscar, as he punched Joey in the arm.

"Ow!" Joey yelled, as he swung back to punch his friend but missed.

"Come on, man. Don't be a pussy! Let's get a little trashed, you know what I'm saying?" asked Oscar as he started to shove the bottle into Joey's face.

"Hmmmm" said Joey. "Fine. Let's get up to my room, you doofus."

Joey unlocked the front door.

"Don't be loud, you shmuck. My parents are sleeping."

"Okay," Oscar whispered with a big shining smile on his face swinging the bottle of whiskey around. "This is going to be awesome," Oscar whispered again, as they tiptoed upstairs to Joey's room.

They got to the room and took a seat on Joey's bed.

"Okay. Let's see what you're made of," said Oscar, as he popped the top open of the bottle of whiskey.

Joey gulped and stared at the bottle as Oscar took a humungous swig that made Joey cower in fear.

"Wooooooo," said Oscar, as he swallowed the large shot out of the bottle.

"Jesus Christ," said Joey. "You're a freaking beast."

"Your turn," said Oscar, as he passed the bottle over to Joey. Joey grabbed an older can of Mountain Mist and looked down on the bottle and the can. He thought twice, and then took a large sip of the strong whiskey that Oscar brought. He followed it by a large swig of Mountain Mist to chase down the taste.

"There you go!!! Even though you needed a chaser like a little bishhh!" said Oscar, laughing.

The look on Joey's face said it all. He wanted to spit out the whiskey, but he also didn't want to let his friend down. So he held in the nausea. "It burns so good."

"That's my boy!" Oscar jumped up and patted Joey on the back to show his sign of approval.

Two shots turned to many shots, as seconds turned to minutes, minutes turned to hours. The two wasted the night away playing video games, which Joey was highly against at first but he became more and more fond of the idea the more drunk he became. They also thought it would be a good idea to prank call people they knew in high school. But one of Oscar's ex-girlfriends recognized his voice, so that soon came to an end.

The night turned to early morning as Oscar and Joey finally polished off the rest of the bottle. Joey had more to drink than he had consumed in over a year. The two got black-out drunk, and both passed out around five thirty in the morning. Oscar fell asleep on Joey's bed and Joey fell asleep in his computer chair with his legs propped up on his desk.

He woke up, still in his spinning desk chair, at eleven thirty with the worst pounding headache he'd ever had. *Feels like an anvil dropped on my head*, he thought, as he looked at his computer and saw that his FaceSpace was up and logged into.

He scrolled down his page to find that he had made a few drunken posts on the God page that he didn't remember until just now.

One read, "Yu don't hav to believe inmee to kno I ixist!"

"What the hell!" Joey said out loud. "Did I really write that dumbass shit?"

The post underneath read "*I* createdd all of dis in six dayz, on the seventh, I searched for hoes with my Bruh Bruh."

Joey's eyes lit up as he could not fathom why he would post such ridiculous things.

The final one read "Fuk you Amber you stupid ass! U missd outt on dating a god!!! I hope u tripp n fall dow nthe strsirs!!@*#"

"Damn, I was a mess last night. Thanks a lot, Oscar," said Joey out loud as he looked over at his friend passed out, snoring, and drooling all over his pillows. *You gross bastard*, Joey thought.

He immediately clicked on the upper right column of his first drunken post and clicked on the *delete post* button. Then he proceeded to do the same for the other two.

"I can't let people think God is a drunk," Joey said to himself.

Joey remembered the post he made about AllTalk and decided to take to Findoo to look up any news on the matter. He typed "ALLTalk" into the search engine. Immediately, 545 related news articles came up, all with similar stories. "Start Up App Company AllTalk Prepares For Shutdown," and "AllTalk Corporations Plan To File Bankruptcy." Another one read, "Investors Pull Out Of

Start Up App Company, AllTalk."

"Holy crap," Joey said. "I can't believe this is happening."

Joey immediately opened up his FaceSpace page hoping to at least balance out the small stitch of guilt that he felt. He went on his God page and began to type out a new status:

How can we change the world for the better?

Joey posted that question at 2:01 p.m. on August 16th. He left his computer for a moment to give people a chance to respond. He felt very horrible about what he had done to ALLTalk. ALLTalk wasn't actually that bad a company, and Joey knew that. But the chance to get back at his ex who shattered his heart was far too good an opportunity to pass up.

He played Ruby Drop on FaceSpace for a while to pass the time as he also thoughts about things he could do to make the world a better place. *Maybe I can help a smaller company rise to the top or something. After all, I did do the opposite,* Joey thought.

Some time had passed before he checked his page for feedback from his followers.

Danny Shillinglaw wrote:

You should start a campaign for saving dolphins. Maybe partner with the Dolphin Rescue Of Paradise.

Pshh, that's stupid, Joey thought, as he scrolled to the next person.

Melanie Peters commented:

> Maybe start a petition to have more hospitals in Canada. The free healthcare is great but it causes there to be an unreasonable amount of waiting and lines. I'm thinking of having to pay for it and moving to Texas anyway. There's this cute guy that lives there.

More and more posts were coming in, one after the other. Joshua Joubert wrote:

> I think there should be a LOT more schools in rural areas. It's always so pressing of a task to get to school.

Tina SuperStarBooBoo Jones wrote:

> There should be a skool JUST for trying to be a celebrity, no what Im saying? Lik, so mofucks cud git famuss in lik a day. That coud be koo rite?

"Fucking morons," Joey said to himself. "Now I see why the flood had to go down. And I thought my spelling was atrocious!"

He scrolled down to the later posts. Maybe some people took longer because they actually used their brains.

Marvin Bolden made a comment:

America isn't in the best shape right now. I think more funding for gyms would actually benefit. As far as the world, I think there should be a LOT more attention paid to churches and their need of easier business benefits. For example, they should get better Internet prices because spreading the word of God should be the MOST important thing and the internet is the best means of doing so. In addition, it'd be smart to provide them a MUCH better price on advertising. It could change the world for the better for sure.

"Seems kind of worth it," Joey said to himself.

Nikita 2Pretty Packard wrote:

I think you should create Internet schools. That way you can employ more teachers. Have everyone in a room and have the best video conferencing software and hardware available. Hundreds of rooms, and make special classes, like college for kids inside their school. Maybe run a course on how to file taxes in middle school? Maybe offer advanced history or current event classes as early as in elementary schools? Just some ideas.

Joey liked those last two posts; they were actual ways that could change the world in his eyes. At least they were good ideas, not something Joey had a harder time relating to and seeing its importance, like helping dolphins even though he wished he cared more about the environment.

He read some more posts and even got disgusted at a few, such as Donald Ramone's, who wrote:

> I think woman's rights have gone too far. I can't even get a girl because they're so full of themselves. If it could be like back in the caveman days where you could grab a bitch by the hair and toss her into your cave and have your way with her, I'd be happy.

"What is WRONG with people? People are fucking retarded and pathetic human beings," he jokingly answered in another voice.

"Don't say *retarded*," Joey quickly added with concern to himself, not exactly liking the word.

As soon as those words came out of his mouth, he clicked on the *Write Post* button as he wrote:

> Everyone, listen. Special needs children in this world don't get all of the attention they need and certainly don't receive the proper care or professionals that are needed. I think we should raise the salary of special needs workers and special needs teachers. Also, their parents should get MUCH higher tax deductions and offered better jobs through companies that can partner with the cause in some way. There's so much more we can do. Any other GOOD ideas?

Minutes later, Terrance Blanding, a teacher from Delaware posted:

> I LOVE this idea! You could also have schools made particularly for special needs children, have three teachers per class and maybe no more than twenty students per room. It won't cost much, being that the amount of special needs children are significantly lower than not. You could even connect all levels of school in one big building, Elementary, Middle, High School, maybe even progress to colleges for them!

Terrance's brother, Lamonte, replied on Terrance's comment because he had been notified with a tag:

> Good idea big bro! They should add a smaller sports league too! Like baseball teams, things easy to manage. This really could change the world.

Joey hoped that people who could do something about these things would see his page and make a change. Not just because he felt a bit guilty about ruining a whole company's progress and hard work, but also because he truly had lost faith in humanity. He wanted to believe there was enough good left in this world that someone else's life wouldn't be as shitty as his. This was Joey's way of giving back. He also had no clue how he could make any of these things happen in real life. So at this point, he knew he was just blowing smoke.

Joey went back to his earlier post about ideas of changing the world.

HugeMunnyDigits, a local rapper from Idaville, Oregon had commented around 2:33:

Ey man, make my alblum goe platnum 2NITEDUDE my G!

Joey replied to the post:

When you can spell platinum I'll think about it.

Joey chuckled as his wittiness had entertained him.

"Well, that idiotic post was my cue to leave."

Joey took a deep breath of air, realizing that most of the responses he would get would be immature and idiotic requests. He reached down to grab the Mountain Mist can from the night before. He took a sip before realizing he was not drinking his favorite soda, but in fact he was drinking his own urine. He had forgotten that when he gets drunk, he would end up peeing in a soda can instead of getting up and going to the bathroom. He used to have a system that he would flick the lid on top of the soda can up, so he would know which one he had peed into. Since he hadn't gotten drunk in a long time, he forgot about the system.

"Yuckk!!" said Joey after he sprayed the piss out his mouth all over the floor.

Chapter Ten
The Book of The Hipster

MAN, WHAT A GOOD EPISODE, Joey thought, as he closed the ViewTube bar. He grabbed some shorts and a wife beater and got dressed. He headed down the stairs and out the door. Joey decided to walk instead of using the car as he was only going a mile to the thrift store and wanted some exercise.

He walked down the street and saw a mom playing with bubbles with her three year old daughter; a rugged-looking man walking his dog as it pulled the owner along.

After about fifteen minutes of walking, he made it to the thrift store, Sadies.

He enjoyed going there just to see what new things they had

that day. For the most part, it was a lot of the same stuff. Some clothes, random fancy jackets, televisions, old computer monitors, a few laptops, some country CD's, and these neat wacky pens. Tons of other things were in the shop, of course, but mostly little trinkets and odd offs. He went up to the counter to speak to the owner, Ms. Andrea Sadie.

"How are ya today, Ms. Sadie?" asked Joey.

"Great. How about you, Joseph?" asked Andrea.

"I'm doin' all right. Amber and I broke up, but other than that, life's great," said Joey.

"Aww shucks, really? I thought you two were so adorable together. Maybe she'll come around," said Andrea.

"Heh, but now I don't know if I even want her to come back around. Like, it hurt when it happened, but I kind of saw it coming, and I think I realized that I didn't even want her that badly. I think the breakup just hurt my pride, I guess. Anyway, do you have anything new today?" asked a curious Joey.

"No, nothing really. Just some new video game that someone brought in. It's called *Vistron*. Some new space-age shooting game thingy. I don't know anything more about it. But you might like it."

Joey laughed and said, "That's not new, Ms. Sadie. But I will buy it off ya though. How much you want for it?"

"Well, I only could give the kid $10 for it. Just give it back, and we'll say deal!" Andrea said while smiling.

"Aww, well thanks Ms. Andrea. Normal tab on credit?"

"Of course! You've never once stiffed me with money, surprisingly. You young kids these days are carrrraaaaazyyy," Andrea said with a smirk on her face.

Joey looked down at his phone, then looked back up to smile at Andrea, and back down again to text.

"Thank you so much, as always, Ms. Sadie. I'll borrow some money from my sister, and I'll have it by you tomorrow. She owes me money anyway."

Andrea looked at him with a more serious face, "Joey, take your time. You know I love you to death. You and your family were there for me when my husband died. So do not even insult me with your nonsense."

"You too, Miss Andrea. I'll always be there for you," Joey said emotionally, as he walked out of the store and headed back down the street to his house where he received a text. It was his carrier telling him that 40% of his data for the month had been used up already.

Hmph, waste of seven seconds.

Joey felt like someone was following him. He looked behind

himself, just to make sure, but no one was there. He got to his house where his sister was hanging outside with her boyfriend who now was no longer allowed in the house.

"Mom know you're outside with Mr. Dick Hard?" Joey said.

"Suck a bag of old man balls, you dork," Jane replied as she held closer to her man's arm, with her phone in the other hand.

"What are you doin' on your phone there?"

"None of your damn business."

Joey looked down at his phone, and saw that he had one million new followers since the last time he checked. He typed in J-A-N-E, and the phone highlighted his sister and showed she liked his page about four hours ago.

Joey smirked upon the discovery, and typed a new status:

> Ladies, respect yourselves. If a man will become intimate with you the first day you two meet, he is most likely never going to be the one you marry.

Joey put his phone in its holster and headed towards the door. But then he stopped and turned toward his sister's boyfriend.

"Hey dude, you may want to think twice about marrying my sister one day since you two are so intimate. Our family doesn't take kindly to mother fuckers who take what they want and, well you get my point. Treat her right, dude. You both are young. If you're going to act like grown-ups, well, then act like grown-ups."

Joey made his way inside and checked the fridge. *Thank God,* he thought as he grabbed a newly stocked ice-cold Mountain Mist from the fridge.

Taking a swallow, he checked his phone at the same time and nearly drowned when he saw a picture of a rather attractive-looking girl. Her name on FaceSpace read Laura Collins. She liked his page, followed him, and sent him a message:

> Hey umm, "God." Look. All of these morons might be remedial but I'm not. I know you're probably some kid or whatever on a computer who made this page up as a joke, but as someone from the outside looking in, and honestly looking for some work, I should let you know the Government is keeping a close eye on your page and you're going to need someone to keep it safe and hacker free. If you're serious about your page and whatever your agenda is, and you need a helping hand, text me.

She listed her number and then wrote:

> It's not a Jersey number. It's New York. Anyway, I think we can help each other. Be smart! ☺

Joey thought, *Maybe I'm feeling a bit paranoid was right.*

Maybe this is a sign. Nah, I'm probably just tripping.

He entered his room and flopped onto his bed. The central air cut on, which prompted him to pull the covers over his head. Joey checked the page to see if it had grown with likes from any more people. Not much of a change today— maybe one thousand new followers. *Perhaps it's reached its peak.* He opened up the page and clicked on his 'Hi' post to read some of the comments.

Alicea Marie:

> *Hi God! I LOVE YOU!!!*

YeVette Derene:

> GOD!!! I go to Church EVERY Sunday with my children Hubert and Olivia. My Husband Hubert comes a lot too! This family LOVES you and always will!

Thomas Linzelle III:

> YoYo! I prayed for the girl of my dreams and I got her! You're the best, God! Now I can quit sniffing pepper!

Huh? Sniffing pepper? This is getting weird.

Boredom struck Joey again so he decided to visit FM Station,

X-Soy Radio's Page.

*I wonder if anyone got that ri...*His train of thought was stopped in its tracks when he saw his father had posted an answer to the giveaway question about what John Mills' Fourth Album was. His dad's answer was 'The Cassidy Disaster.' Under his answer was a reply from X-Soy Radio, *That's right! You were the first to answer correctly! You are now able to message our like page to claim your prize!*

Joey, taken back yet not surprised at all, couldn't help but start laughing. "My dad is ridiculous."

His laughter turned to sadness as a flash of Amber jumped in and out of his mind. Thoughts of loneliness settled in as a different image flashed Laura Collins. *Hmm, maybe I could try and have her help me. Working with her may be a good way to keep my mind off of Amber.*

He wrote Laura:

Hey, so I've been thinking. Let's do it.

She wrote him back, almost immediately as if she was waiting for him to write her:

Cool! Your God page is based out of New Jersey. I can do my work from here but it'll take a lot longer. If we could meet up that'd be best. Actually, call me! You have my number. Or get it from my website.

Joey quickly went to her website, found her number, and dialed it.

"Hello?" a voice uttered from the other side, a lot more pleasant than Amber's.

"Hi. Umm. Look, I'm not really sure what to make of this all," said Joey.

"It's all good," replied Laura. "It's not everyday someone who has more than forty million followers on a FaceSpace page and gets an offer from some hacker chick who needs money."

"Well, how does this work exactly?" asked Joey.

"Okay, man, basically this is how it goes. Your FaceSpace follower count is over 45 million. That's celebrity status, so you have a significant amount of power over mindless people who don't stop for a split second to think that God definitely doesn't use a computer. The government isn't going to ignore this. Chances are they're on your case already. Pretty soon it'll be to the point that they know where you live. That's where I come in. I can keep your system safe. I'm good at this shit," Laura explained.

"How much money are we talking?"

"I normally charge about $100 a month, sound good?"

Shit, I don't have that kind of money... I don't have any *money,* Joey thought.

"Yes, that sounds great. What's the next step?"

"You're in New Jersey, right? I'm in the city, so we're only about an hour or so away from each other. If I'm able to work with your system, it'll take about forty minutes to finish. If I work from here, it'll be more like days. You could either pay my way or bring your laptop here," said Laura.

"I actually use a desk..." said Joey.

"Desktop. I should have known anyone who'd make a God page is probably some weirdo introvert who doesn't get out much. Geesh, enjoy some nature for once! But that's hard to do with a desktop. Maybe you'll get yourself a laptop?" she asked.

"Yeah, I'll work on that. Are you against me coming to you? It'd probably be easier that way," said Joey.

"That's fine. You can either get yourself a laptop, like any young in-tune person, or I can actually put my code on a flash drive that you install on your dinosaur of a computer, and you should be good to go."

"I think it'd be better if I came down, so I'll do that. I'll call you when I'm on my way."

Joey ran downstairs to talk to his Mom.

"Mom, I'm visiting my friend in New York City for a little bit. I got $20 from Tyson for gas, so you don't have to worry about me. Bye now!"

But before he could hastily leave the house, his mother said, "Woah. Wait, son, I've never once ever known about you having a friend in the city."

"Or any whatsoever!" Jane yelled from the other room.

"Want Mom to know any other secrets?" Joey asked, threatening his sister.

"What else would we need to know?" his mother asked.

"Sorry, Mom. I need that info for blackmailing purposes."

Joey made his way out the door, exiting before his mother couldn't ask any more questions.

Ugh! Again! Joey thought, as he ran back inside the house and up the stairs, ignoring his mother's added attempts at conversation. He grabbed his car keys, went back downstairs, still ignoring his mother, and out the door.

On his way into the city, Joey stopped by the CompuNerd store at the mall.

He headed inside and Courchesny was there working. He headed straight to the aisle labeled Computer Accessories and grabbed the least expensive Bluetooth keyboard he could find. Of course it was CompuNerd brand, but Joey's idea was to use it with his computer, so he could avoid bringing his desktop to the meeting or having to pawn it at Palms-Out Pawn for a laptop.

*Thirty five bucks...Christ...*Joey thought, while walking back to the counter.

Courchesny, with that same bright smile on her face, greeted Joey, and began to ring up his keyboard.

"Gee, we see you a lot here, huh?" she said.

"Heh, yea, I'm sort of a dork," said Joey. "I love anything with a wire or anything that can plug into a wall."

Courchesny laughed, as she put his items in the bag and scanned his gift card for the balance.

"Yeah. I'm the same way. Have a good day! Nice seeing you again."

Joey smiled at her and scratched his head. "It was nice seeing you. Have an awesome one."

Courchesny was a looker, all right. At 5'3, she was slightly heavier than thin, but in good shape, with short blond hair. She wore glasses, and a pen in the pocket of her tennis shirt. Realistically, she was right up Joey's alley. But Joey was on a mission to meet a cute little hacker from the city. There was adventure in this; there was travel. Joey just figured this girl was a lot more fun to pursue. He made his way to his car and sat while he programmed the new keyboard to his phone.

"Alrighty, I love technology. Even a simpleton could do this shit."

The task took him all of thirty three seconds. He cranked up his car. After two revs, it started right up. He made his way to the highway, which was right off the parking lot, and sped towards the city via the Jersey Turnpike.

After approximately 98 miles of weaving in and out of traffic, and about an hour and forty minutes later, he arrived in New York City. Once there, his trip soon came to a slower than slow halt.

Wow, this traffic is just insane.

Joey looked around for a place to park; he would deal with a ticket later. Even if he found somewhere to park, he'd still have a hard time getting to the spot as the streets were completely congested. *Well, I'll be here for a while.* He pulled out his phone and punched in Laura's number.

After two rings, she picked up.

"Hello?"

"It's Joey. I'm here in New York, and all I can say is…WHAT THE EFF?"

JEFF YAGER AND SKYE BYNES

"Let me guess. You're stuck in traffic?" asked Laura.

"Exactly. This is insane," Joey said.

"You said you'd call me before you came here, soooo, sorry? I thought I should have warned you sooner to take a train instead or something. Where are you? Like what street or landmarks are you by?" asked Laura.

"I see a 'Great Purchase' on my left, and a Q-Store to my right," said Joey.

"You're still a bit away from me as far as driving. Try and park near the Billy's Shoe Store. It's about half a block up and has a huge garage. Three dollars will get you eight hours of parking time," said Laura.

"I can actually see it. The speed I'm going at, I'll probably be there in about half an hour," Joey responded.

"Trust me, it'll take longer than that. Tell ya what. I'll come look for you. What kind of car are you driving?" she asked.

"A Blue Accord. I'll have my lights on, so you can spot me easily.

"No problem! I'll be right there. Give me like...fifteen minutes. You're close, but not that close."

After about four minutes of waiting, he picked up his phone and checked the God FaceSpace page. He pondered and then began to make a post. It read:

> We have airplanes, we can send a picture through
> air, we've been on the moon, now can New York City
> offer a Goddamn Air Taxi service?
> #TRAFFICSUCKS

Joey pulled forward a bit, as the traffic let up a little, and then
he took a sip of some half-day-old Sir Frizz he had in the car.

He turned on the radio and "Crump it Up" by Big Silly Zack
was on. He immediately turned the radio off and pulled up
ViewTube on his smart phone. *I wonder what this girl is like in
person. I hope she's not too nuts.*

He searched ViewTube for newly-uploaded videos that he may
not have seen. He saw the Tribe of Circuitry channel and clicked
on it.

Still stuck in traffic, Joey was enjoying an episode of Geek
Tweek about turning an everyday computer into a great-looking
beast of a machine, when he saw a woman resembling the online
photo he had seen of Laura waving at him. Joey waved back and
rolled down his window.

"Hey," he yelled, as Laura walked over to his car, opened the
passenger door, and hopped in energetically. She showed off every
tooth in her mouth as she smiled at Joey.

"OMG, Hi! So you're the famous, 'God', huh? People are so stupid! It's still cool, though. I feel like I'm in the presence of royalty," she said, not being able to control her laughter.

"Ha, ha, yeah, royalty," Joey said sarcastically, as the traffic began to let up a bit, just enough for him to advance a few more feet. "So, hey. I got a Bluetooth keyboard for my phone. Can you work your magic with it?"

"Can a tranny bang you in the tooter?"

"Fair enough." Joey tightened his butt cheeks. "So, have you ever heard of Geek Tweek?"

"Oh my, Joey! I love that show! Did you see the episode where the guy had them totally hook up his grandmother's laptop? They put a freaking Life Save button on the keyboard for her. That was so cool."

Laura reached into her backpack for a Chocolate Twin Bar.

"That was too cool. I loved the episode when they, hold on." Joey paused to pull up a bit more, clearing his throat. "Sorry, I *loved* the episode when they took the kid's desktop and put in a fish tank for liquid cooling — I wish I would've thought of that."

"That was the one where the kid had cancer, right? He always wanted a pet fish, so I guess it made sense. His mom had to have set that up," Laura said.

"David Mesley is the man. If I had that type of money, I would have the single best computer on the face of this planet."

"Tell me about it. I have a low-end Sildec PC. I've been trying to save up and get a CompuNerd PC. They're not too expensive, but they're *so* good for the money."

Joey replied, "I actually have a CompuNerd PC, so I know what you mean. It's a good, middle of the road machine. Good enough for movies and videos. I can't really game on it, but I don't really play games that much anyway."

"According to FaceSpace, God enjoys some Pissed Off Penguins and Ruby Drop!" Laura responded with a "gotcha" expression on her face.

"OK, you're creepy as shit," said Joey.

They both laughed. Joey was a bit more sarcastic, as he was indeed a bit creeped out by the fact that she had basically stalked him.

Bleh, it's actually kind of hot, he thought. He looked at her with a slight smirk.

"Have you ever watched 'The Hand That Kills'? It's like my favorite show ever," Laura said.

I think I'm in love, Joey thought, as they pulled closer to Billy's Shoe Store.

"So yeah chica. We just happened to have the same favorite show. You sure you're not stalking me?"

"No, I'm not stalking you! That's so cool! No one I've known even *knows* what that show is! Only my nerdy friends have ever heard of Geek Tweek, but other than that sort of stuff, horror films are my absolute favorite."

She and Joey engaged in an intimate eye lock for a brief moment.

"I also love a good chick flick from time to time, of course, like *Sing and Love. Great* movie," she added.

"Ugh, I can't watch chick flicks," said Joey. "They're so...chicky."

Joey and Laura both laughed.

"Oh, look," she said, pointing forward at the traffic letting up and allowing them to move about 150 meters.

They both let out a sigh and locked eyes once again in amazement of how much they were alike.

"Let's get in an episode of Geek Tweek. That'll help pass the time."

"Sounds nice," Laura said as she put the passenger seat back a bit.

They searched for a random episode that they both couldn't

remember watching the first time and landed on an episode called "A PC for a PC." In that episode, a newly-fostered child named Phillip Charles got his first computer.

They watched as Phillip got his very first computer, which was a high end I.Q: Exile. The initials I.Q. were for the founder of the company, Imran Quincy. These computers were the top of the line, the computer everyone wanted and talked about.

By the time the eight-minute episode ended, they had advanced to Billy's store. As they pulled into the garage, Joey looked at the gas tank icon and realized he was almost on empty. He took out the three singles from his pocket that he had planned on using for gas. The gate opened and let them into the parking section. After another six minutes of driving around the parking lot, they finally found a spot.

They hopped out of the car and began to walk towards Laura's house. On the way, they passed by a Burger Joint and a less than happy look formed onto Joey's face.

"What's wrong?" asked Laura.

"Nothing. Just a bad experience at BJ. Don't really wanna talk about it."

The bright lights of the city had grabbed Joey's attention, mixed with the fact that he was hanging out with an amazing girl.

Having someone to share this moment with just made the cake that much sweeter. *Why couldn't Amber enjoy these things, enjoy his company and who he was, not what he had and how he was doing according to her standards?*

Joey and Laura were walking side-by-side when she tried to trip him, but he was too quick.

"You're good. I trip everyone," said Laura.

"You haven't tripped a god," said Joey.

"Oh, yeah?" Laura stuck her foot out once more.

"Yeah," Joey said, as he tripped over Laura's foot, but catching himself before falling too far.

"It looks like I can trip anything, even a god."

Laura reached into her bag for a second Chocolate Twins bar.

"Looks like you can."

Joey was impressed with her wittiness.

After a few more minutes of walking, they arrived at her place, which had a large stone stoop in front with an eight-foot stairwell. She opened an unfinished, oddly-colored, pink door and they entered her part of the building. Her apartment was a nicely decorated three bedroom with posters of trees and plants everywhere. There were a few dream-catchers, at least one candle on every shelf, a big shelf of books, and a 52" flat screen TV in the living room.

"Wow, you have a very nice place here."

Joey was amazed at what he was seeing.

"Thanks. It was a lot of hard work," Laura said with a slight look of regret in her face.

"You must've had some awesome jobs, or one awesome job for a very long time."

"So where's that phone and keyboard of yours?" asking Laura, changing the subject. "This won't take long."

Joey removed the phone from his pants pocket and pulled the keyboard from his backpack.

"Here ya go. They're already programmed."

Joey handed her the phone and keyboard.

"As if it would matter if they weren't."

She stuck out her tongue.

"I'm computer savvy," said Joey, "but you're on a whole other level with this hacking stuff."

Laura sat on a couch and began her work. Joey sat next to her, trying to see what she was doing.

"You know, if you want to know what I'm doing, you can ask," she said. "I'm thinking of giving you a discount. You're far too cool. I wouldn't even feel right charging up the full fee. It's like two seconds of work for me. Let's say $70."

There was a mixture of glee and business in her eyes.

"Well, I'm grateful that you're willing to help me out." Joey was feeling a bit relieved even though he hadn't yet pointed out that he was completely broke.

"There's a property here called IP Firewall. Basically we're setting it so that it'll change its name every time you re-connect to FaceSpace. So make sure that you go on your page just about every chance you get, or you can actually just refresh the page once in a while. Let me just set these, and *done*! All I have to worry about now is, once a day, to make sure that I update the Firewall's definitions so that they can't follow the pattern it uses to block. A.k.a, it changes the language they speak so hackers or other computers can't just follow your IP's changes that the firewall uses to take effect," she explained.

"Oh?" Joey responded as his face turned from completely confused to just sort of confused. "I think I get it," he added.

"You'll get it," she said, laughing a bit. "After a while, it'll be like riding a bike."

"I'm sure. Maybe to you."

Joey felt a bit more insecure than normal. He grabbed his phone and keyboard and then threw his keyboard in his backpack.

"That was a lot quicker than I thought it would be," Joey said.

"I've done it a zillion times. You'll owe me seventy bucks at the end of this month, OK?"

"Cool."

Joey scratched his eye with his pinky nail in an attempt to hide what he thought would resemble an obvious look of guilt.

"Have you ever been to the city before?"

"I was supposed to come for a school field trip once, but I was sick."

"You didn't want to go?"

"Gee, how'd you guess?"

"I used the same excuse not to come here when I was younger. I grew up in Winsted, Connecticut. It's the 117th smallest town in the state."

"Let's have a quick session called 'Get to know you time,'" Joey suggested. "I ask you a bunch of favorites, you answer and ask me a question back, and we go back and forth."

"I believe that I should use every second of my life wisely. I have one life. I'm not trying to waste it with silly tradition, so how about we do this? I tell you everything that defines me to me, and you do the same."

"Deal. I'll start. My name is Joseph Kennedy Taylor. I'm 26

and I'm currently unemployed. I'm Black and Irish. I like nerdy things, like computers and horror films. I've been to four horror film conventions in my life, and they've been some of the only times I've enjoyed myself being outside of my room. My favorite number is six, and for some reason I love the letter 'I.' My favorite color would be black, and I've lived in the same house since I could remember. I love 90's alternative rock and absolutely loathe this new age pop bullshit. I think the system is the worst it's ever been, by choice, and hate that everyone will stomp on you to get to, and stay at, the top. People are selfish, and sometimes I feel that the only way to get somewhere in life is to be just as selfish. At the same time, I love people, for the most part. It's just hard to trust anyone nowadays. Oh, and I don't do many drugs, drink, or smoke."

"Alrighty. I'm Laura Candice La'Rae. I'm 22, self-employed, and with that comes various forms of income including hacking, web protection, and selling my own brand of anti-virus software, which you should pick up, by the way."

"As soon as my subscription of Horus Internet Management Pro runs out," Joey replied.

"I also go on this website called 'Seven-Dolla-Holla' where people do random things for seven bucks. My particular service on that site is to offer a sexy-sounding narration of any three paragraphs. Most people end up paying me like 500 dollars for books and stuff. It's the best paying gig I have. Not many people out there are looking for website protection these days. Most people end up going out to California for business and what not. Anyway! I have four brothers. No sisters, and yes...I'm the youngest. I'm Irish and Italian, and I'm a *total* hipster. My parents being total tightwads made me that way. But hey, I dig it. I like being the odd one out — makes me feel special. I don't have a favorite letter, but my favorite number is nine, and color is red. I also hate how the system works, but I twisted it in my favor instead of complaining about it like some people," Laura explained.

She chuckled and punched him in the shoulder playfully, yet firmly.

Laura continued, "I like old acoustic style music and, for some strange reason, I love Hip-Hop. I'm a weirdo. Most about me you can just tell by looking around my house. Otherwise, if you ever want to know anything else, just ask me. I'm an open book! Now, come on, let's show you around the city!"

They headed out of her house, back down her old-style stone stairs, and into the main strip.

"The city has a lot of stores, you'll see, just all in one place. There's a Great Purchase on that corner down the street. You can't see it yet, but there's a Sindy's BBQ, over there, way down there. You can barely see the store, but look up."

"Woah," Joey exclaimed, as he looked up and saw a huge Mall-Smart Super Store sign.

"They sell just about any and everything there from food to freezers to store it in," said Laura. She quickly went on to say, "Now check out the strip over here to the left."

Joey looked at where she was pointing and saw different shopping spots, some he'd seen, but most of which he hadn't.

He quietly read the signs that were easily visible to him as Laura said, "Waltons Pharmacy, Scrubby's Shoe Shining, Play Spot."

The walk to Billy's Shoe Store parking lot seemed shorter because of their talking and sightseeing. They soon reached Joey's car and leaned against it, continuing their talk.

Laura adjusted her net cap. "You know what, Joey? You're really, really cool. I've never met someone who..."

Joey cut her off by planting a kiss on her mouth.

Laura was a bit shocked, since the kiss seemed to come out of nowhere, but she was shocked in a good way. She gazed into Joey's eyes, as she battled over her decision as whether or not to ask him to take back the kiss or do it again. He had connected with her like no one ever had and wasting time with the whys and the don'ts weren't her thing.

Instead, she gave into temptation and grabbed him by the head and pulled him in for another kiss. A few minutes went by, and they continued to make out like a couple of teenagers. Joey, whose breathing had now picked up tenfold, rushed his hands into her shirt, holding her by the waist as their tongues relentlessly massaged each other's. His hands moved across Laura's back and down the inside of her pants, caressing her cheeks. Her hands went behind his back and then to his chest as she let her passion move her limbs.

She was truly feeling an out of body experience. Her emotions overtook her, as she took Joey's shorts and pulled them down roughly. Not even taking the time to loosen his belt, she grabbed his manhood while continuing to shove her tongue down his throat. Joey calmly moved her off and went into his car, returning with a condom.

Laura took the condom and tossed it behind her. She pulled 'him' out of his Chet branded boxer briefs and went down on him just enough to get it hard and wet. He then picked her back up to her feet, and roughly turned her around, bending her over the trunk of his car. He picked up her skirt and slid her panties out of the way, and before she knew it, he had, in a very quick fashion, entered her.

It had been a while since she had experienced intercourse, so it hurt at first. But quickly, it turned into certain pleasure and her grunts soon turned into moans. Joey got harder and harder, as her voice was a lot sweeter-sounding than Amber's, a pleasant turn on for him.

Their movements quickened as he pumped harder and harder. Joey then placed one hand on Laura's shoulder, and one on her waist as he continued to thrust himself inside of her. Her moans were getting louder and more passionate. She backed up, took him out, while holding onto Joey's shirt, as she turned to face him. Now she sat on the trunk of his car as Joey looked around to make sure no one was coming. He then went back to performing the deed. Now facing each other, they moaned in unison as he reentered. They started kissing, and then Joey moved to her neck, where his lips began sucking. Unaware to them, a family walked through the lot but fortunately they didn't even notice the two and their very public display of extreme affection.

Joey held Laura down by the arms as his pumping got faster and he got even harder. He then grabbed a hold of her hair as she climaxed and released a moan that echoed throughout the whole parking lot.

As he got closer and closer to 'going,' he began to suck her neck even harder than before. The closer he got, the harder he sucked. Hitting the spot faster and harder than he ever had in his life, he released his seed deep inside of her. He took his lips off of her neck and noticed he had branded her with a huge hickey. He held onto her waist, like a true gentleman, and helped her slide safely down from the car until she was standing on her feet.

"Umm. Wow. That was...godly," said Laura, as she smoothed herself out, pressing her hands across her body to straighten out the wrinkles. She then wiped a small bead of sweat from her forehead. "You do know, I'm not charging you anymore, right," she added. "I just fucked the creator of the fastest growing page on social media today who just happened to have a massive God complex."

"You have no idea what a relief hearing that is," Joey said, laughing. "Don't be mad at me, but I honestly didn't have the money right now."

"No shit. You told me you were unemployed. I put two and two together."

"Thanks for making me feel stupid."

"Hey, you're no better for trying to play me like I'm stupid," she answered with a slight attitude.

"Fair. Fair."

Joey pulled up his shorts after undoing and redoing his belt.

Laura looked towards the far end of the parking lot to see that the street looked unreasonably clear. "Hey, you gotta get out of here. Your time isn't nearly up, but the street is kind of dead. If you don't go now, you'll be stuck here for hours."

She planted a huge kiss on Joey's lips. "Now get out of here before the traffic picks up. Trust me. I'll visit very, very soon."

Laura bit her lips and bid farewell by placing her hand on his chest, saying, "You were very cool and nice to me. It's been a long time since I've felt that."

We all like to feel loved and even sometimes just wanted. This girl taught even me that there's good somewhere in this world.

Joey held on to Laura's gaze as he got into his car. He pulled away, watching her in his rearview mirror until she was out of sight.

Laura turned toward her building. *What a scumbag,* she thought, smiling a smile that seemed impossible to get rid of. *But a nice and hot one. You don't get that hell of a combination every day.*

Chapter Eleven
The Book of The Law

MEANWHILE, OVER ON 24TH Street and Sixth Avenue in Manhattan, Special Agent Kenny Owens was waiting in line at the same hot dog stand he'd been going to for the past three years. He got to the front of the line and greeted the vendor he saw about five times a week.

"Ernie! How's your day going today, my friend?"

"Not bad, Ken. Another day, another dollar," Ernie replied, the same way he did every other day. It was his favorite line.

"I'm glad to hear it," said Agent Owens.

"We getting the usual?" Ernie asked as he began to reach down to grab Kenny two hot dogs, accompanied by a can of Diet Sir

Frizz. "Here you go,"

Agent Owens handed Ernie a five dollar bill. "Keep the change."

"Thank you, sir. You are too kind. Have a safe day now."

"You too, Ernie."

Agent Owens walked away from the hot dog stand and headed back towards I.S.I. headquarters.

Special Agent Kenny Owens had been with I.S.I., which stood for Internet Security Intelligence, for over ten years now, and he planned to retire there. He started his career soon after Y2K. Kenny always told himself the next form of terrorism America would face would be through the world-wide web.

I.S.I. was a special agency that specialized in cyberterrorism. They worked directly with the F.B.I, C.I.A, N.S.A., and local police departments as well as with state troopers and sheriffs. Most people had never heard of the I.S.I. because they were a private organization that worked solely online. It had grown over the last five years into a super agency, responding to all of the crime that occured online.

Many in the agency considered Kenny Owens to be some sort of super-agent, always going above and beyond, able to find inside scoops and leads that others in the I.S.I. could never catch to break cases. He seemed somewhat smug and a bit big-headed after he solved a case the F.B.I. was working on for years involving the Italian Mafia in Brooklyn. In 2008, Kenny infiltrated an online database that worked as part of an Internet black market, where gangs and Internet outlaws would sell, purchase, and trade illegal products. But more specifically, it was involved in cocaine being smuggled in and out of all five boroughs of New York City.

After a yearlong investigation, Agent Owens finally had enough evidence to raid a large business meeting of Italian mobsters, which resulted in over ten arrests of some of the biggest gang members in the city's history. He was promoted after that large bust, and put on a pedestal in the agency.

Agent Owens stopped next to a large fountain in the courtyard of a hotel on 24th Street and Eighth Avenue. He sat on the ledge of the fountain where people had thrown coins when making wishes. He ate his two hot dogs and pulled a magazine out of his briefcase. Owens began to read the magazine when his phone started to vibrate. He put on his Bluetooth headpiece to answer the call.

"Owens."

"It's Rick." Rick was Agent Rick Caruso.

"Hey Rick. How can I help you?"

"I didn't mean to interrupt your exquisite dining festivities. I assume you're about to chow down on a couple of dogs?"

"What's going on, Caruso?"

"We've been picking up some unusual chatter involving a FaceSpace page. It might be nothing, but I thought you'd be interested."

"You got my attention. What's the chatter about?" asked Agent Owens.

"You have to see it for yourself. I'll shoot you an email. You're gonna be happy with the find. Give me a shout after you've seen it, and let me know if you want to take the case."

"Will do. Talk to you later," said Owens.

Kenny clicked *end* on his cell phone and took a large bite into his second hot dog, followed by a swig of his diet Sir Frizz soda.

He then clicked on his email icon to see what Caruso had sent him. It was a link to a FaceSpace page. He continued to click on the link provided.

The God page Joey had created came up.

"What is this, a joke?" Kenny said out loud to himself, seemingly confused. "Caruso must be losing it."

He closed up his phone and returned to the magazine he was reading.

Agent Owens opened up to page thirty and started to read an

article about his favorite country music singer, Billy Brooks. The country star had two hit singles and a music video with sixty million views on ViewTube. Owens liked Billy Brooks because he wrote songs that touched Kenny's soul.

He had gone through a tough divorce a few years ago that led to his ex-wife taking both of his children. His ex-wife had taken him to court and the judge gave him every other weekend to see his son and daughter. On top of that, he had to pay child support when all he wanted to do was see his children and be with them and his wife. But Kenny had a bad history of being verbally abusive to his wife, although he never hit her, but she finally left him. He was about to lay his hands on his wife a few times, and the last time, when she felt he was really going to do it that time, was the final straw.

He hadn't found a new love since, sleeping only with prostitutes every now and then. He once had a good heart, but over time, he turned into an angry middle-aged man who let his emotions get the best of him.

Agent Owens finished his lunch, crumbled up the tin foil the hot dogs came in, and threw his trash into a garbage can on the corner.

He started walking towards the I.S.I. headquarters only a few blocks away. On the way, he passed by a group of loud-mouthed high school kids. A couple of them were on skateboards and being disruptive. They cursed each other as well as strangers that walked by.

Agent Owens stopped in his tracks and walked over to the group of troublesome boys. A beautiful blonde woman walked by the group of kids, and they started to shout and to pester the pretty lady. One kid shouted, "Let me see the way you move them hips girl!"

"Hey!" yelled Owens, as he approached them.

"What do you want, ya old fuck?" asked one of the high schoolers, trying to appear tough.

"Old fuck?"

Owens grabbed the boy by his belt, and yanked him out of the group. The boy tried to pull away but Kenny shoved him to the sidewalk. "Do you even know who the hell you're talking to?"

"Who are you?"

Agent Owens pulled out his I.S.I. badge. "I'm somebody you kids don't want to fuck with!"

"You're a cop?" asked one of them.

"In a sense. I'm a cyber cop."

"Huh?"

The boy struggled to stand up to join his buddies.

"You boys get the hell out of here before I take you downtown to the sheriff's office. Stop acting like jackasses and get to school!" exclaimed the angry Agent.

The boys scurried away, running down the street. Some nearby civilians who had watched the scene unfold began to applaud. Owens waived to them and continued walking back to work.

As he entered the front lobby, Kenny greeted the girl at the front desk, whom he had a crush on for a few months now.

"Hello Denise," he said, as he signed the sign-in sheet. Here was a top-secret organization hidden in Manhattan that still used a paper sign-in sheet that its special agents and staff had to sign whenever entering or leaving the building. They also had a special access key card that only I.S.I. authorized users could obtain, which one would assume would have made such manual sign ins superfluous. And they were, except the director insisted on maintaining the appearance of a low-tech operation.

"How are you today, Agent Owens?" asked the delightful young woman.

"I'm just fine, Denise, and yourself?"

"Great, as always, sir."

"Denise, please call me Kenny. Or Ken. Or whatever you like

really. Anything except 'sir.'"

"Okay, Kennnn-ny. Have a great day."

"You too Denise. You too."

He walked across the lobby to the elevators and took one to the top floor. Before he could enter the floor number, he had to slide his special agent key card that granted him access to their floor. The elevator began to lift, moving floor to floor, until it reached the tenth.

The door opened and Agent Owens walked down a long hallway that stretched a quarter of a football field. There were offices and cubicles squeezed into every spot along the way. He walked past different agents, mostly men, with a few women special agents as well.

He finally reached his office, the 16th one on the right, between Special Agent Jenkinson on one side and Detective Watts on the other. Kenny walked into his office, trying not to bother anybody, as he sat down at his desk. He kicked his feet up on it and looked out the window. He had a beautiful view of the New York City skyline, especially at night in the fall when he was getting off work and the sun had started to go down.

He opened up his laptop and turned it on. Owens looked over to the picture of his two kids that he had on the wall of his office.

He smiled as his computer started.

Owens first checked his e-mails, and saw one that read: "Urgent from Agent Caruso: God File."

"This oughta be fun," Owens said as he opened the e-mail.

> This isn't a joke. I think we have some new cyberterrorist on our hands, Ken.
> Go to www.facespace.com/god
> Just check that shit out. Think we got a new big fish on the horizon.
> Talk to you later,
> Caruso.

Kenny clicked on the link and saw the page. Similar to other cases when he was first told about them, he didn't think much of what he looked at initially. But then he read through some of the tens of thousands of posts and comments. He still couldn't put his finger on what he was looking at or why Caruso thought this was something worth investigating.

Owens was a Christian who went to Bible study class as a young kid. Religion was very important in his family growing up. He immediately saw the God page as being a little off-putting, but not cyberterrorism or anything like that. He couldn't see how he could make a case out of it. His initial take on it was that it was the work of some Internet troll who created a page to get views and attention. Nothing stood out to him in particular, but as he continued to read 'God's' posts, he found his almighty AllTalk bashing post. "Now we're getting somewhere," said the Special Agent. "I've got my eye on you, whoever you are," Owens said out loud.

He continued to creep through Joey's page. "What are you up to?"

Agent Owens was mesmerized by what he was seeing on his laptop screen. Nothing made his blood boil more than the idea of Internet terrorism and crime. When he started a case, it was like beginning a puzzle that he would never give up trying to figure out until he solved it. Owens thought that this time, Caruso might actually be on to something with this one.

Chapter Twelve
The Book of Spaghetti

OSCAR INVITED HENRY, Chris, Tyson, and Joey over for spaghetti and meatballs. His aunt wanted to cook for them and they all arrived around seven o'clock. Chris and Tyson arrived together. When they walked in, Tyson walked over to Oscar's aunt and gave her a kiss on the cheek, then proceeded to smack her butt.

"Hey, man," yelled Oscar. "Not in front of me!"

They all laughed as Oscar's aunt continued to cook for the group. While they waited for the meal to be served, the group sat down in the living room to play Oscar's new BZK400 game system. He already had two games, a football game and a first-person shooter with futuristic guns and intense flying vehicles. The game had been hyped for months, encouraging people to buy the new system along with the latest games. Oscar said he wanted it because of the graphics and engine. Joey never understood why his friends were so obsessed with video games. He still went along with it, so he wasn't an outcast, even though his friends were all outcasts in their own way.

"Do you need help in the kitchen, Erica?" Tyson asked from the living room.

"No, I'm okay, *mi amor*," said Erica as she poured her homemade tomato sauce onto the spaghetti.

"Hey, Oscar! Can you come watch the stove for me? I have to use the bathroom," said his aunt.

"Ughhh , no! I'm playing Father of Arms! Tyson go help out your wifey and watch her food for her," said Oscar to Tyson.

"*No problemo,*" Tyson hopped up to go watch the food.

"Thank you, baby," said Erica before she kissed Tyson on the lips.

"Anything for you, Mama," Tyson said, as he looked over to Oscar in the other room and gave him a wink.

"Nasty Fucker!" yelled Oscar.

"This is freaking awesome," said Chris. "I need to get me a BZK400 of my own."

"They're pretty sweet, aren't they?" said Oscar.

"How many controllers do you got?" asked Henry from the love seat on the other side of the room.

"I got two, but let me play for a little on the full screen before we have to do split-screen," said Oscar. "I want to enjoy my brand new baby."

Oscar kissed his wireless controller.

Erica got back out from the bathroom and joined Tyson in the kitchen just as he tasted the spaghetti out of the cooking pot.

"Hey you! You wait until we all eat!"

"Whaaa?" Tyson had a mouth full of spaghetti noodles hanging down to his t-shirt.

"Want to be a bad boy? You can now set the table for everybody."

"Oh, man, fine," said Tyson.

Tyson then proceeded to take out six forks, plates, and knives for everybody. Then he started to place them on the table in front of all the chairs.

"Thanks, handsome," Erica said to Tyson.

Once Oscar got a couple of rounds in, he let his friends play the new video game.

"Anybody want a beer?" asked Joey.

All the guys looked over at him like he was crazy.

"What," said Chris.

"Joseph Taylor wants to have a beer? Henry, look out the window. Are pigs flying? I need to know."

"Shut up, man," said Joey.

"You should have seen him the other night," said Oscar. "We had a bottle of whiskey between the two of us. Joey was messed up."

"As were you," said Joey, as he got up from his chair.

"Yeah, but you should have seen some of the stuff you were posting on FaceSpace that night. I was cracking the hell up. Oh and that prostitute we prank called from BuckPages? You had me rolling on the floor, my man! That was classic."

Oscar cracked up as Chris and Henry started to laugh with him.

"Did I hear that Joey got drunk?" Tyson shouted from the kitchen, while he was holding Erica with his arm around her, kissing her neck. "That's awesome BROOOO!"

"Yeah, whatever," said Joey.

"Oscar, you got any beers?"

"Check the garage. We should have a case of Blue Bark out there."

"Sure."

"If I have some, grab me one," shouted Oscar.

"Me too," Chris and Henry shouted in unison.

Joey went to the garage and there was indeed a case of Blue Bark Beer sitting next to a fridge that hadn't been plugged in for years.

He walked back inside to join his friends, tossing Oscar, Chris, and Henry their beers. Tyson screamed from the kitchen "Hey, where's mine!?"

"I forgot about you, biatch! Go get your own," said Joey, as he cracked open his bottle.

"I'll remember that, homie," said Tyson, as he walked by and winked at Joey on his way to the garage.

"Boyssssss," called Erica. "Dinner is ready!"

"Be right in, auntie," said Oscar.

He and his friends couldn't take their eyes off the high definition graphics of 'Father in Arms.'

Oscar finally paused the game as the crew stood up and rushed into the kitchen. The smell lingered throughout the house, making all of their stomachs growl simultaneously.

"Smells amazing, Erica" Chris exclaimed.

"Thanks Chris," said Erica. "I get my cooking skills from my grandmother," she went on.

"Well, tell her thanks too!" said Chris.

They all sat down with their beers in hand, ready to scarf down as much pasta as they could.

Tyson was the last to sit down with the group, and pulled out a sketchy tin can with holes in it.

"Guys, when Oscar asked me to come eat tonight, I asked my momma for this special seasoning," said Tyson. "It's kind of like a special sea salt, pepper, lemongrass, and herb blend rub. It's really amazing. If you guys want, you should try it out." Tyson tried to pass around the seasoning.

"Oh, so you don't trust I can cook or something?" asked Erica.

"Baby, you know I know you can cook. I'm telling you to try some of this stuff. I, for one, like to put a lot of it on my food. It puts you in a trance, I'm telling you, it's that good!"

"Eh fuck it, I'll try it," said Joey, as he reached over to table to grab it.

"That's what I'm talking about Joe, Joe," said Tyson.

Erica passed around the large bowls of spaghetti and meatballs, as well as a side of salad, and her very own cheesy bread. The boys were looking forward to eating her food because Oscar was always raving about his Aunt's cooking.

Joey poured some of Tyson's Mom's Special seasoning over his pasta, and a little too much came out onto his plate. "Oh shit!" he yelled.

"It's okay, man," said Tyson. "You can never have too much of the stuff."

Tyson grabbed the special concoction from Joey and poured some seasoning onto his own plate.

"Well if you're doing it, I might as well try it," said Henry, as he shook some seasoning on his pasta.

Chris decided to follow the others and try it. Even Erica wanted to see what all the fuss was about.

"I don't need any. I love my auntie's food. I don't need nothing on it. It's perfect the way it is," said Oscar.

"Suit yourself," said Tyson, as he took a huge bite of his dinner.

"This is actually pretty good," said Joey.

"See, I told you," said Tyson.

"Na, it's because of Erica. These meatballs were cooked to perfection. Great job, Erica," said Joey.

"Oh thank you, sweetie," she said. "And your mom's seasoning ain't that bad, Ty."

"Bangin! Just bangin," said Chris.

"All right, fine. Let me get some of that Tyson crack," said Oscar, not wanting to feel left out.

He poured the last of the seasoning on his food. Oscar had a problem with feeling left out and always had to try to accommodate his friends. He always tried to impress them when they were fine with him anyway. He was still self-conscious beyond belief.

"I'm glad we're all eating dinner," said Henry. "It's so cool."

"I agree," said Oscar. "We don't do this enough. Let's make this a habit, guys."

"Totally," said Joey.

"This seasoning has a funny taste to it, Tyson," said Henry.

"That's the lemongrass," said Tyson, as he took a big bite of pasta and slurped up his noodles from around his fork.

"Could you be any louder, you cow," asked Oscar?

"Yes I can. Ask your aunt."

"Shut the hell up, before you get kicked in the teeth," said Oscar.

"He didn't mean it," said Erica. "He's just playing, right sweetie?"

"Right."

"This is a great dinner," said Henry. "Thank you for cooking for us, Erica." Henry took a big bite cheesy bread, followed by a large gulp of his beer.

"I like doing it," said Oscar's aunt. "You guys are fun to hang out with."

"So what you guys want to do tonight besides play video games?" asked Joey.

"Great question, champ! What should we do tonight?" asked Oscar, as he dug into his pasta.

"Really. I just want to play Father In Arms. That shit is so fun," said Henry.

"I think we should find some girls that want to hang out. Maybe we can play beer pong," said Chris, as he drank his beer and finished up his plate of food.

"Let's have a good night, boys! Let's have an adventure," suggested Joey.

"I agree, man," said Oscar.

The boys and Erica finished up their food, and brought their dishes to the sink.

"You can do the dishes, Joey," said Tyson. "I had to set the table!"

"No problem. That's fine," said Joey, as he started to wash the rest of the food off the plates and into the disposal, before washing the dishes and silverware with dish soap.

While Joey cleaned, the other boys and Erica went into the living room to play the new video games Oscar bought.

As Joey was just finishing the last dish, he started to feel a little funny. He stared at the sponge in his hand. He was wiping the dish in a circular fashion, and before he realized it, his hand was wiping the air. "Woahh. What's happening?"

He could hear the boys in the other room reacting to the video game, watching Oscar play a couple rounds of Father in Arms on the brand new BZK400 he had just purchased for a little over four hundred dollars at Hallmart.

Still staring at the sponge, Joey walked into the room where his friends were playing the game.

"Guys? Is anybody starting to feel a bit strange?" asked Joey.

"Yeah, my stomach is full as hell, and I'm stuck on this couch over here," said Chris.

"No, really guys. Something's happening," said Joey, looking around the room, which had started to moderately vibrate. To Joey, it looked as if the walls were breathing in and out but with small inhales.

"Oh, it's starting to hit you already, Joe," said Tyson.

"What's starting to hit me?" Joey noticed that the colors on the television had brightened before his eyes, and he started to feel like he couldn't stand as he dropped into Oscar's bean bag chair.

"Oh shit," said Oscar. "What the hell did you do?"

Oscar started to feel his face, starting from his chin to his ears.

"I thought it would take a little bit longer to hit us," said Tyson. "I didn't know these mushrooms were that strong. Hold on, oh snap."

"What mushrooms?" asked Oscar, as he stood up from his chair and looked at the television. The graphics seemed to be popping out of the screen. The soldier across from Oscar's character in the game looked at the screen and Oscar felt direct eye contact with the soldier.

"Woahhh!" Oscar yelled.

"You guys know that seasoning my mom gave me for our dinner tonight?" asked Tyson.

"Yes!" said Chris.

"What the hell did you do, Tyson?" asked Henry, who was starting to feel a bit funny as well.

"Well, that was really my own seasoning. And by seasoning, I mean grounded up some magic mushrooms that I purchased from my homey, Mike. You know Mike who does those amazing paintings?" said Tyson.

"What the shit, fuck," said Joey, as the mushrooms really began to hit him hard.

At that very moment, he felt as if something had invaded his body and had taken over every cell. "HOoooolllllyyyyy Smmmokkkkkkeeess. Wwwhhhhhaaaat did youuu do tooooo meee?" he asked, as everything around him started to slow down. He could hear every single heartbeat pounding through his chest by the millisecond.

"You freaking nut case," shouted Chris.

"I think I can hear my leg hair growing," said Erica, as the effects of the hallucinogenic mushroom begin to hit her like a bulldozer. "This is insane!"

She stood up and walked over to Tyson. "You are so in trouble."

Erica fell into his arms with a smile on her face.

"Wow, now she is messed up," said Oscar.

"This is really happening right now at this very moment," said Joey. Oh em gee." *Oh my God. I can't believe I just said "Oh em gee,"* Joey thought as he felt like he saw a bug crawl on Chris' face.

"Now I really want to play video games," said Henry.

"Me too, actually," said Joey.

"You are a real dick head for doing this," Oscar said to Tyson, as the overwhelming sensation of the trip started to take its toll on Joey's best friend.

"Well, at least we now have something to do tonight," said

Tyson.

"This isn't exactly what we had in mind. Mind. Mind! Mine! Mine," said Joey.

He couldn't believe what he was witnessing in the room around him. All of his best friends were tripping out.

"This is nuts guys," said Chris. "I've never done this before."

"I have," said Oscar. "But nothing this strong."

"How long is this supposed to laugh," said Joey, who realized he meant to say "last," but didn't and now he didn't care as he walked around the room slowly with his hands elevated in the air. "Look guys. I'm hovering."

"Dude, you totally are," said Chris, but then he turned to Henry and said, "Joey's not really hovering, you know that, right?"

As the hallucinations became more real and intense, the boys and Erica formed a conga line and danced to the music playing from the music channel on the television. The sound was blasting through surround sound with the bass hitting them in the face every time it bumped.

The boys danced and laughed, and Erica even invited a few of her friends over, as the night turned it into a small party. Two pretty ladies in their twenties came over to have some fun. They played rap songs and tried to recite the lines, messing up almost every time. The boys had a few freestyle battles, two of which turned into shoving contests and almost fist fights. At one point, Joey took to his phone and went on FaceSpace. After long discussions about what he should post while tripping balls on magic mushrooms, he came up with his first post. He clicked the *write post* button on his phone and began to type:

> Thou Shall Not Be A Pussy
> GIVE HER THE D

Before he clicked *publish post*, one of the girls, Tanya, fell on his lap while she danced to the EDM song that blasted through the house. He clicked *publish post*, and proceeded to kiss the astonishingly pretty girl in his lap. He was high out of his mind. She looked like a fairy princess to Joey who had, in fact, tripped balls.

Later in the night, Joey went back to his FaceSpace to post more status updates for all his worshipping followers to see. At that point, he had just shy of forty seven million likes/followers on his FaceSpace page for God.

"People like having people to text and tag on FaceSpace because it's easy," he wrote. "Real life human interaction is the truly hard part."

Joey clicked 'Publish Post'.

Before they all ended up crashing out, sprawled all over the place, Joey got to second base with Erica's friend, Tanya. Ultimately, he fell asleep next to the toilet with his pants down his waist because he was in the middle of pooping when he finally passed out for the night. Long story short, it was a very unique and weird night for the crew.

The next morning looked like a scene from one of those *Hungover* movies. The boys had turned Oscar and Erica's house into a jungle. Cups spilt everywhere, packs of bologna almost empty lay on the floor with trash everywhere, one broken lamp, couch cushions scattered on the floor from wrestling matches the boys held late at night while coming down from the mushrooms. Oscar's wooden table lay broken in the center of the living room next to all the couches.

By two o'clock in the afternoon, Joey had awoken from his deep sleep where he had still been hallucinating in his dreams.

He got up on his feet and walked over to the room full of wasted souls passed out all around the living room and to the kitchen floor.

"Wow, last night got crazy," Joey said to himself while the rest snored and dreamt away.

He looked down at his phone and saw he had one missed call from his mother from the night before, as well as tens of thousands of notifications from the posts he made. He opened up his phone and looked at a few notifications before he came to the last post; he recognized that it wasn't he who posted it.

The post read:

> Joey likez to smear penut butter on his penis and have his dog lick it off Jajajaja – #HACKED BY Oscaaaaa.

Joey read the post out loud to himself before freaking out and deleting it altogether. He walked over to Oscar's lifeless sleeping body and started to kick his friend.

"Wake up, you piece of crap!"

Joey continued to kick and nudge Oscar.

"Okay, okay. I'm awake. What's up!?"

"Why the hell did you hack my phone and post that crap on my page?"

"I was just playing around. Last night was crazy. I don't even remember what I posted."

"Well your dumbass said my real name on the God page. Joey!"

"Oh, so? Who cares?"

"What if I can get in trouble for this? I need to be private. You have no idea, man!"

"Sorry. My bad."

"And out of all the things you could have posted to 47 million people, you post that dumbass shit."

"I thought it was funny, I guess."

"I don't care man, fuck you. You fucked up. Don' talk to me, you prick."

Joey stepped over the other sleeping bodies and made his way out the front door.

"My bad!" yelled Oscar, as Joey opened the front door and slammed it shut.

Chapter Thirteen
The Book of Disloyalty

JOEY SEARCHED THE INTERNET for any jobs hiring in the area. But he couldn't find anything he was qualified for so Joey turned on the television. On came one of a dozen or so all news channels. He was about to change the station when he heard the on camera reporter say "This just in...

"Authorities are investigating a new controversial FaceSpace page for 'God.' Apparently, it has been causing a lot of trouble. Recent posts made by the person running this page has allegedly caused AllTalk, a startup app company, to go bankrupt. The company has been forced to downsize and many at the corporation have lost their job. Also, other posts made by this anonymous FaceSpace user have inspired followers with posts such as:

'God has many faces and languages but I don't speak Arabic so please stop sending me messages in Arabic.'

"Other posts have urged people to prepare for the coming revolution, whatever that means.

"Join us later for more information and updates as this story develops. Is this social media god someone we should look up to for inspiration, or is he in fact somebody evil waiting for any moment to use his new found power to do something awful? Who knows?"

Then the reporter turned to another camera and said..."and now..."

"What the hell!" Joey turned off the television and picked up his phone to call Laura. The phone rang a few times before she finally answered.

"Hey, Joe. What's going on, babe?"

"Have you seen the news lately? They got my page on there, Laura!"

"No, I haven't seen it. Just calm down. We're going to be okay, Joe. Trust me. You haven't done anything really that wrong. People use their pages all the time to slander large corporations and famous people."

"I'm freaking out over here," said Joey.

"Calm down. You're gonna be fine. I won't let anybody find out who's behind the profile. I promise."

"I hope so."

"Trust me" Laura reassured Joey.

"Okay."

"I gotta run, Joey. Hit me up later and we'll talk."

"Okay, beautiful," he said.

"Bye, Hun."

Joey pressed the 'end call' button, and put his phone in his pocket. He got up from bed, walked out the bedroom door, and made his way to the front door. He was just about to open it when his mother stopped him.

"Joey!" said Mrs. Taylor.

"Yes, Mom. What's up?" asked the troubled Internet troll.

"Where are you going, sweetie?"

"I need to clear my head and go for a walk."

"Oh, my poor baby. Is it because you and Amber broke up? It's okay, son. We all go through heartbreak."

"No, Mom. It's not that. I can't really explain it. I just need to get out of the house for a few minutes."

"O.K son. Be safe."

"Okay Ma. Love you."

Joey stepped outside and started walking towards the street in front of his house. He walked down the block and thought long and hard about everything that was going on in his life.

He made his way to the next street and fiddled with his thumbs before taking a seat on a rock. He pulled out his phone and looked at it.

"This Internet shit is getting crazy," he said aloud.

After thinking to himself for about five minutes, he stood, stretched, and began running. He ran down the street. Even with his knees beginning to buckle, he kept running. He stopped for a second to stretch out his leg as well as both of his arms, and then he ran again.

Joey didn't run often, but for some reason, he decided he needed to. He ran as fast as he could, not breaking a sweat for a couple blocks. He didn't stop for about ten more minutes until he got too winded and needed something to drink. He turned around and headed back home as he walked and breathed loudly, and then he started to jog the last few blocks till his parent's house.

He walked through the front door and headed to the kitchen. His sister was playing games on her phone in the living room, lying on the couch with cartoons on the television set behind her.

"Woaahhh! What the hell were you doing?" asked Jane, as she looked up from her game and saw her brother breathing hard and panting.

"Just had to do some running, that's all."

"That's hilarious. You *never* run."

"Well, I needed to clear my head. Now mind your own business."

"Okay, God," snickered his sister, as she continued to laugh at her older brother before going back to her cell phone game.

Joey opened the refrigerator and grabbed a cold, bottled water from his mom's drawer on the bottom of the fridge. He unscrewed the cap and began to chug it down like he had never swallowed the beverage before.

"Ahhhh," Joey said to himself.

"You sure are thirsty," said Jane.

"A-huh."

Joey continued to finish the bottle of water.

"Maybe you need to find a girl or something, to get rid of that thirst, if you know what I'm saying," said his sister.

"Shut up, Jane. I'm already talking to one. And maybe even more. So worry about your damned self."

Joey stormed out of the kitchen and headed up to his room,

running up the stairs, taking three steps at a time. He was so tired from running like that in the first time in forever that as soon as he got into his room, he dropped to his bed and sprawled out.

Moments went by, and Joey couldn't stop thinking about his life. His phone beeped, but he didn't want to get up. He saw that it was Oscar, so he decided to answer it anyway.

"I'm sorry," said Joey, "This is not the snitch hot line, for snitches".

"Ha Ha. Very funny. What's going on, man?" asked Oscar.

"I don't want to talk to you, dude," said Joey.

" Why?" Oscar asked.

"Cuz you're a dumbass and could have gotten me caught."

"Dude, it's not like that," said Oscar.

"Oh yeah. Then what is it like?" asked Joey.

"You should be mad at Tyson. He's the one that laced our dinner with fucking magic mushrooms!"

"Tyson was only trying to make us have a good time. You had to take it to another level."

"I'm sorry, bro. I didn't mean to piss you off. Was just trying to be funny," Oscar tried to explain.

"Well, it wasn't funny. Truthfully, I am disgusted with you," said Joey.

"Chill, man."

"Nah, Oscar, you're a freaking dumbass."

"You know what, man. I wasn't gonna say this. I was gonna keep it a secret not to hurt your feelings. But fuck it man, you want to be an asshole, then so can I," Oscar said.

"Oh yeah? What's that?"

"Remember a few months back when Amber took a weekend trip with her 'cousin' or whatever the hell she said?"

"Yeah. So what?" asked Joey.

"That 'cousin' wasn't really her cousin. It was me. She and I took a trip to Philly, and we got a hotel room for the weekend."

Joey's face turned bright red as he sat up in bed and started to feel a bit queasy.

"You're playing, right?"

"Naa. You can even ask Chris. Me and Amber got it in all weekend," said Joey's backstabbing friend.

"You piece of fucking crap. I hate you," Joey acclaimed.

"You never told me how fine that ass was, bro. Sucks you just lost it forever. I wonder if she'll pick up my phone call."

Joey clenched his fists to stop himself from throwing his cell phone across the room but that would have only hurt him, not his friend.

"If I ever see you again, I'm going to break your fucking jaw," Joey said, in a loud, slow, yet agitated voice.

"Yeah, right. You're a little punk bitch. All that power behind a keyboard. But in reality, you would get dropped on your big fat head, Joey."

"Fuck you, man. You're going to be really sorry, you asshole!" said an angry Joey.

"Fuck you, Joey. You started this."

"I did? You posted on my page some dumbass corny-ass shit. Now you're telling me you smashed my ex when we were still together? Fuck you, you piece of scum. Watch out."

Joey clicked the *end call* button and this time, he couldn't stop himself as he threw his phone across the room. It hit the wall and fell to the floor.

"Ah," screamed Joey.

He grabbed a pillow and put his face in it before screaming again at the top of his lungs. Joey was angrier with his so-called best friend then he ever thought possible.

He then turned on his television and started flipping through the channels before stopping on the Worldwide News Channel (WNC). There was a special report about the rise of the infamous God page on FaceSpace. Joey turned up the volume.

"This page is being used in blasphemous ways," said the anchorwoman. "Just the other day the creator of this page took it upon himself to ask his followers/fans/believers, whatever you want to call them, to stop using the popular new app for smart phones, AllTalk. We are not exactly sure why the person behind this page has a problem with the app company. But within a day or two, word got around, and even investors began to pull out of the company. Millions deleted the app at the drop of a hat."

"Uh oh," said Joey as he kept on watching for a little while longer.

"We're not exactly sure of the reasoning behind this FaceSpace user's actions, but we are sure of one thing: his power and control should not be taken lightly. He isn't the first person to try to take matters into their own hands. But this is the first story of this magnitude, so we should not take the actions of this page lightly. He could be like the hackers, such as Monogamous who hacked the BZK400 online system last year, as well as the most recent elections website, and most infamously for the world healthcare website.

If you have any information on the identification of who is behind the 'God' page on FaceSpace, please call our Anti-Crime hotline at the number at the bottom of your screen. Anonymous tips are okay and a small reward is being offered for those who can provide any real information on their identification."

"That's not too good, is it?" Joey said to himself.

"Who's to say the guy behind the God page isn't just like any of these other cyberbullies," said one of the experts seated next to the anchorwoman.

WNC has no god damned idea what I am about. Trying to group me in with Monogamous? I'm not some petty hacker. I'm tryna make a change, Joey thought.

"What the hell am I going to do?" Joey asked out loud.

Then he remembered what Oscar had said and started to get angry again.

"Fuck Oscar."

Chapter Fourteen
The Book of Power

JOEY PACED BACK AND FORTH from his bed to his desk, and back again, over and over. His paranoia was getting the best of him.

What the hell, man? Oscar put my name on it. Someone could have seen that. They could have counter-acted her anti-hack by now...Anything could go wrong!

Joey stopped at his desk to take a large swig of Mountain Mist. He then sat down in front of his computer and pondered how he could stop this, once and for all, and more importantly, how quickly. An idea sparked in his head as he quickly hit the already available 'Write Post' button and started to type:

"EVERYONE! STOP WATCHING WNC!

They tell lies and are trying to ruin the minds of everyone WITH THOSE LIES! Purge your minds, and STOP WATCHING THAT TRASH!"

Posted at 2:20 PM on August 22nd

That'll fuckin teach 'em to fuckin' fuck with me!

Joey's anger dissipated into a nice mixture of satisfaction.

Within minutes of his post, a WNC representative commented, "That won't work 'God.' We here at WNC are a dedicated and well-respected team of newscasters. People have believed in us a lot longer than they've believed in you, whoever you are behind the keyboard. We are warning you, please stop this now."

"Hmph," said Joey, as he confidently ignored the post. He then took another swig of his favorite soft drink, as he grabbed his phone to make a call.

"Hello?" answered Laura.

"Hey. So I'm still a bit shaken up. Is there a way you could come to Jersey? I think I need you," said Joey.

"Sure," Laura sighed. "I'll be there as soon as I can. Oh my God..."

"What?" asked Joey.

"Are you just crazy nuts, or freaking coo coo? You made a post about WNC? You're going to make this worse!"

"Ugh! I know, but it's the only thing I could think to do to calm the situation down. If I get away with this, then I get away with this, but if I let them out me, I'm doomed for sure," Joey tried to explain.

"I'm on my way, OK? The next train leaves in less than twenty minutes, and it normally takes me fifteen minutes to get there. If I hurry, I may be able to make it, bye! Talk to you when I'm on the train."

The word "train" barely left her mouth as the phone beeped, indicating a disconnection.

Joey went straight back to his page to see if WNC said anything more. Although they didn't respond yet, a post replying to their comment read "Yea right! Screw you WNC! We're behind God ALL THE WAY!"

A smile arose on Joey's face, as he felt a bit eased about his situation. Moments later his mother screamed out, "JOEY! COME HERE QUICK!"

Joey bolted down the stairs and into the living room. "Check this out," she said.

Joey looked at the TV. WNC was on, and Joey's ears listened

in, as he joined in on the newscast in progress.

"...page is out of control. He or she, whoever, has already managed to put the company AllTalk in a bankrupt state. Who knows when they'll get their business back up?" said reporter Matthew Jackson.

"This 'God page' is certainly rocking things for everyone who's in his, her, its, path. Just minutes ago the page urged followers to stop watching WNC, an obvious reaction to our coverage of the page," added the reporter to the right, Don Cooper.

"Yes, quite obvious," said Matthew. "Who is this cyberterrorist? We need to stop him at all costs. We've been told that Cyber detectives are on this. The F.B.I. has gotten word. I mean, this is now a federal matter! He's put a company out of business, and he's now attacking a major news corporation. It'll only be a matter of time until we catch this monster and put an end to this."

Joey's mother turned to her son. "Who would make a page like that? Even I liked the page, your father too," she said. "This guy says a lot of good things, but he's bold too. He said some good things. Earlier he made a post about how to change the world. He had great ideas, as did some people who answered. This guy is like...an actual God. The ones who put him down suffer, and the ones who need him and cause no harm are loved by him. I like his views and ideas; I just don't like some of his decisions. But, isn't that how we view the real God? Some things hurt people, but it's all in good karma," his mother went on.

Joey was deep in thought until he heard his name.

"Joey?" said his mother. "Did you hear what I said?"

"Oh, sorry. I was just thinking of how crazy this whole 'God page' thing is. This guy must be a real moron. I don't have a FaceSpace myself to like his page, but I'm sure he's not as bad as some people seem to think he is."

"I don't think he's bad at all. He's just very harsh and opinionated," said his mother.

Without saying anything else, Joey headed back up to his room to be alone and ponder the crazy world he'd gotten himself in to.

Wow, I'm fucking famous, Joey thought, as he sat on his bed to rest his nerves.

Hours went by, as Joey just laid in his bed and thought about his situation, before he drifted off into a deep sleep.

After what seemed like hours later, he got a phone call from Laura. *Finally!* Joey thought to himself. He was amazed at how much he missed Laura and how much he had grown to care for her even though they had only just met.

"Hey you," he said.

"Hey there, you crazy person. I was watching some Nerd Bird on the train and forgot to give you a call, my darling."

"It's okay, really. What's Nerd Bird?"

"This show about how these two brothers from England that try to find a nerdy chick that'll date them both. It's hilarious. They think she'll help get them through college, both with grades, and ladies," Laura said.

"Either way, sounds like some funny shit. So where are you?" asked Joey.

"I'm going to be hitting Camden in like ten minutes. Don't worry. I know where you live," she said, confidently.

"How? I knew you were a stalker!" said Joey, laughing.

"You know for someone so smart, you are pretty stupid. Just kidding. I have an IP hack directly from your pages outgoing connections. A.K.A. You're on my GPS, bitch!" Laura smiled, as she enjoyed the one up she had attained over Joey.

"Sorry. You taught me a little bit, but I'm no pro at this hacking shit," said Joey.

"Have the door unlocked. Be there in a bit!"

"Will do."

The conversation ended and Joey looked at his phone to see how much time had passed.

Holyhell...it's 3a.m. Joey thought, as he excited, knowing that he would soon have company of the female variety. He went to his computer to turn on some music. He typed ViewTube into the URL column and threw on a playlist named 'When playing Solitaire,' — a good variety of songs not containing lyrics. Most of which were calm for easy thinking. Joey went through different phases where he could only listen to instrumental music.

He didn't open up Solitaire and instead opened a FaceSpace game that he got an invite from another page he had liked named 'Alternative Rock, Rocks my Rocker!' The game was called 'Musical Savior' where a popular song from an artist would play and you would tap to the corresponding notes on your keyboard. You could also connect it to a guitar, bass, drum set, microphone, and flute that you could plug into via a USB port.

Pretty cool. I wonder if they have any good songs. At first, he did horribly, always off beat, late or early in his timing. But after some time passed, he got the hang of it. *This is super fun.*

Joey was still playing and getting better and better every round he played until he got another phone call from Laura.

"I'm outside!"

"Ok. I'm coming. Everyone's..."

"Asleep, so keep it down. Yeah, yeah," said Laura.

Joey chuckled. He loved her sense of humor and wit. He headed downstairs from his room, through the kitchen, and opened the front door. Laura immediately jumped on him, with her legs wrapped around his waist, and then planted a big juicy kiss on his lips.

"I can't believe this shit you're getting me into," she said. "You better be glad I like you. If we get through this without going to jail, you better love me FOREVER!"

She planted her feet on the floor and looked around. "I can't see much, but it looks like a nice house."

"Yeah," Joey said. "My parents work hard. They like nice shit. So yeah."

"Heh, who doesn't? So where's your room?" Laura asked.

"Whoa. Slow it DOWN! I just met you!" Joey said, imitating one of his favorite battle rappers growing up.

"First of all, be quiet," Laura shushed. "People are sleeping."

Joey smiled at her, and pointed his head towards his room, invitingly. He walked up the stairs, with Laura following close behind. Joey plopped on his bed, and Laura closed the door behind her quietly, then lied down next to him.

"How the hell are we going to get away with this, God?" she asked. "Any ideas?"

"That's what I pay *you* for!"

"You don't pay me, remember."

"I pay you with this dick."

"Oh shut your sexy ass up." They shared a passionate kiss, which undoubtedly led to other intimate variations of events.

The next morning, around 10a.m., Joey and Laura were laying in bed, on their phones.

"You know this whole thing was supposed to be just a big joke," said Joey. "Something stupid to enjoy. Something to offset some boredom."

"Well, I hope you're *enjoying* yourself now."

"Yea, something like that...I'm definitely not bored anymore, I'll tell you that." Joey said.

Joey sat up. "Be right back."

He walked downstairs to grab himself a Mountain Mist, when he noticed a note on the fridge.

It read: 'Hey sweetie, we were going to let you know yesterday, but you were asleep. Your father and I were offered a vacation from his job, and we jumped on it! We'll be back in about a week. We love you, Joey. We left some money for you taped to the back of this.'

Joey checked the back of the note and saw only the tape, "JANE!" Joey yelled, suspecting his sister of taking it.

"WHAT?" she answered, as Joey noticed the loose money lying on the ground.

"NEVERMIND.I LOVE YOU!" he shouted, trying not to feel too stupid.

"Uh huh. What do you want?" she answered.

"Can't a brother tell his sister... Never mind!" Joey grabbed his drink and headed back upstairs.

He entered the room to see Laura sitting at the edge of his bed.

"Hey, just updating my definitions for the firewall," she said abruptly.

"That's good. That's good. Did you want something to drink? Sorry, forgot to ask."

"Do you have water? Otherwise, I'm good. I don't drink soda."

"Sure, one sec." Joey ran downstairs to grab a bottle of water. "Here you go," he said, tossing it to her.

"Thanks for finally thinking of me."

"Thanks for trying to make me feel guilty."

Joey kept checking the God Page to see if anything new had been posted, then switched to a news site to see if there were any other developments there. He looked worried, as he jumped back and forth between sites, just waiting for something to go horribly wrong.

"Stop," said Laura. "If something is going to happen, we can't do anything about it. I'm telling you. We're safe. Let's go for a walk or something. Get your mind off of this."

"Sounds good. Let's do that." They headed down the stairs and out the door, then cut to the right and started walking down the street.

"Do you like thrift stores?" Joey asked while wrapping his arm over her shoulder.

"Like??" Laura asked with her eyes popping out of her head. "No, I love them! I was going to ask you if you go to thrift stores too, but thought you'd think I was lame."

"That always happens to me," said Joey, smiling. "Like, when I think something, someone else thinks it too. Normally happens with people I'm truly connected with."

She smiled back. "Yeah, I always thought that too. It's as if when we think, it's like a WiFi connection, and sometimes they can interfere with each other and thoughts get joined. Just my theory."

"I could see that being true. I mean, isn't life already crazy enough? To know there's a God, or something up there that made sure we had oxygen, and that we were far enough from the sun so that we don't burn. But just close enough so we don't freeze. It's amazing."

Joey rubbed his fingers through his hair.

"Anyway, I want to bring you to a friend of my family's," said Joey. "Her name is Miss Sadie. Very nice lady. Her store doesn't get a ton of business, but it's a nice thrift shop. She's a smart lady. If she actually made some money out of that place she'd hook it up for real."

They were just around the corner from said shop.

Laura began to ponder, "Miss Sadie. Sadie's. Didn't you make a post about that almost a week ago or something?"

Joey smiled. "Heh, I almost forgot I did that."

They turned the corner and saw a large group of people outside of Sadie's Thrift Shop.

"No freakin' way," said Joey.

They walked closer and saw that the shop was so full of customers others were forced to outside. Joey made his way inside with Laura, telling those in line that they worked there, so they wouldn't think they were trying to cut in.

They walked inside to see not only Miss Sadie, but her niece and nephew working in there as well. They had newer items to sell now, TV's, projectors, newer clothes and video games, jewelry and other items that were never available in the store before.

"Hi Miss Sadie!" shouted Joey. "I see things are goin' great here!"

"VERY! You going to sit there and talk or are you going to help this rush?" she asked.

Joey and Laura nodded to each other, as they both began to help out. As the crowd got larger, things started to get rowdy, even to the point where people began to steal things. An eight-year-old girl was shoved to the ground by an older nasty man who was trying to check out the newer video games that the store had available. The parents of the poor little girl were off looking at items, and the girl started to cry. Laura called the police on the man on her cell phone, and then purposely delayed his purchase to give them time to arrive and haul him off.

Two and a half hours went by before the rush subsided. Now, with just a few customers in the store, Joey and Laura were able to talk with Sadie.

"Thank you two so much," said Sadie. "We were handling it okay, but it was definitely becoming a headache that could have gotten out of hand. The day after you left, business picked up here. And the day after that, it was a mad house. I've never made so much money in one day before," Sadie said.

Joey smiled, knowing what he did. "I'm so happy that this place turned around. It was honestly getting depressing around here with the lack of customers."

"Yes, child. It is a true miracle," said Sadie. "I thank God for what he's done for me."

"Well, give yourself some credit too, Miss Sadie. You do well here," said Joey, realizing she had no idea that in this case, it was Joey and not 'God' who was responsible. Still, he didn't want her to give him credit.

"Well, hey," continued Joey. "We only came by to say hi. I didn't expect it to be this busy. We have to head out."

"Fine! Nice seeing you, Joey! Here." She handed him a one hundred dollar bill. "I appreciate your help today, and it's the least I could do."

"Thank you so much. You have no idea how much this helps me," Joey said.

"Yeah. Your mom told me you weren't working anymore. Good luck with finding a new job, if you want you can work here!"

"Let me get out of here, before you try to trap me," Joey said, laughing. "Love you Miss Sadie!"

"Nice meeting you," said Laura, as the two walked out the door.

"So, where shall we break this Benjy?" Joey asked Laura.

"You keep it, Joey. I'm fine, and you need it." Laura placed her hands in the pockets of her baggy dark green cargo pants.

They made their way back to Joey's house, where they were interrupted by Joey's little sister.

"Who's the girl? Way too pretty to be *your* girlfriend," said Jane.

"She's my," Joey looked at Laura for some sort of hint. "...friend from elementary school, before you were even born. For your information, she's totally in love with me," said Joey.

"Yeah, right," said Laura. "Maybe. Okay, I am." Laura smiled with embarrassment.

They made their way into Joey's room and got right into bed, where they cuddled and watched Geek Tweek on Joey's streamer box. Spooning, they soon drifted into a deep sleep in each other's arms.

The next few days were spent with Laura, working hard to keep intelligence and police off of their backs. He kept up with his God page, making sure things weren't popping up that could result in him getting in trouble. He became a bit smarter than he had been with his newfound power. He knew he had bigger fish to fry, and now it was about protecting himself, Laura, and his family. Otherwise, they spent their time doing what they loved, watching horror movies, their geek shows, having lots of sex, and making each other laugh any way they could.

But the good times they were having would soon come to a halt. It had been exactly one week since the first WNC report went live about Joey's 'God' page. Erica called Joey's phone.

"Hello!? Joey?"

"Hey, what's up, Erica? I hope you're telling me that Oscar fell off a mile high rock."

"No, and I wish you two would patch things up. Anyway, have you heard about this 'God' page that's all over WNC? Oscar said you'd probably know something about it, and laughed. Do you?" she asked.

Joey disconnected the call and turned on the news just as they were reiterating the story, as it was the top headline.

Two new reporters were on the screen at the time, Patty Lynn and Jeremy McGriff.

"Where are those two assholes that were shit talking my page?" Joey asked Laura rhetorically.

Laura shrugged her shoulders and let out what seemed to be a mandatory "Ionno".

Patty said, "Hi, it's me once again, Patty Lynn and my partner, Jeremy McGriff, filling in for the team of Matt and Don who have left due to recent budget cuts. But we wish them both the best in their future endeavors. We will be here, however, every day to bring you the news the best we can.

"In a new update, the FaceSpace controversial page for 'God' has been attacking various brands online, and now even our very own, WNC. How long until this page ruins *your* business? We need to stop liking this page and following it. It's ruined so many people's lives already — workers from ALLTalk losing their jobs, Matthew and Don are gone from here, possibly due to this nonsense. Now, we over here at WNC are calling on you the viewer to unlike this 'God' page. The user behind this account obviously doesn't care about others and their families. We must put a stop to whoever is behind it."

The camera shifted to Jeremy.

"This is definitely a problem for the ages," said Jeremy. "Where a single person behind a computer can cause such a fuss about anything he or she chooses. There may even be a whole team on this. We're still making attempts at finding the source and shutting it down. Even the best cybersecurity isn't helping, but we WILL get to the bottom of this."

Joey and Laura held each other and then stared into each other's eyes.

"Joey, we're fuckin' UNSTOPPABLE!" Laura screamed, barely able to stay in her shoes.

Meanwhile, unbeknownst to this pair of Internet fugitives, Special Agent Owens was also watching the broadcast on WNC in New York City. He then went to Joey's God FaceSpace page to check out what was going on. Maybe there was a clue or something he could use to help him solve this case that had been getting under his skin. He noticed Joey's posts about boycotting both WNC and AllTalk, and began to look at all the comments. He even stalked some of Joey's followers that had blindly agreed with him on many of his posts.

"Self-righteous prick," Owens said to himself louder than any normal man would. "He thinks he really has some power, doesn't he? And that he can do what he pleases, no matter the consequences."

Owen searched the social media pages, looking for anything else he could use against this online vigilante.

His job offered a special type of software for the more popular social media sites. He used it to see if maybe something was posted and deleted, anything that could help him. He noticed one post made recently that was since deleted.

"Hmm, Joey's your name, huh?" Agent Owens said to himself, as he scratched his chin as a look of hope made its way to his face.

Chapter Fifteen
The Book of Money

JOEY WALKED DOWNSTAIRS and was heading out the door when his mother stopped him. She put her hand on Joey's shoulder.

"Joseph Taylor, hold on one second. I'd like to speak to you for a moment."

"What's up, Mom?"

"Joe, I'm getting worried about you. You haven't worked in so long, and I'm worried you're getting too comfortable with not working. Nobody will judge you if you work at a fast food restaurant or do landscaping outside."

"Mom, I'm looking for something. Don't worry. I will have a job very soon. I promise," said Joey, as he opened the door.

"Because your father and I want you to meet a new girl. We know you are hurting after breaking up with Amber, and you're not going to find a new girlfriend moping around the house on your computer all day. You know that right?" asked his Mother.

"Mom, I'll be fine. Besides, I already met somebody new. She's really nice. Her name's Laura."

"Oh, that's so nice. When will your father and I get to meet her?" asked his somewhat surprised Mother.

"I don't know, Mom. She was over the other day. You were at work or something," said Joey.

"Okay, sweetie. I'm glad you're moving on. Do you need to borrow twenty dollars or something?"

I really could use it right about now, Joey thought before saying, "No I'm okay, Mom. Thanks for offering, though."

He kissed his mother on the cheek and walked outside to his car. He opened the door, got in then put the key into the ignition. When he turned his car on, he saw that he was very low on gas, right above the empty line. He drove down the block to the nearby Letz gas station and put seven-dollars-worth in his tank. He used his credit card, praying to God, ironically, that his card would let him get the gas he needed.

It did, and Joey got back into his car and took off out of the station. As he drove, he called Tyson, putting it on speakerphone so he could drive and talk at the same time.

"Joeyyyy Theeee Gawddd!"

"What's goin' on, Ty?"

"Just hanging out, coolin."

"Word. Did you hear about me and Oscar's fight?"

"Yeah, I heard a little bit. Y'all need to stop fighting yo. You're gonna break up the crew, you know that."

"That cocksucker had sex with Amber while we were still dating! I don't think I'll ever forgive him."

"I know what you mean, dawg. I've had a lot of background in this field. Most women are hoes, dawg. When you learn that, you'll be okay."

"Na, bro. The fact that Oscar did that shit is not cool, not cool at all."

"Well that's between y'all. What you doing today?"

"No clue yet. Tryna figure out a way to make some money. Some guap. I got bills to pay, and my parents are starting to hound me about getting a job. I wouldn't be surprised if my dad kicks me out any day now, really," said Joey.

"Ahhhh...a money mission. I may be able to help you with that. I always got some ideas to stack some paper you know," Tyson said.

"What you doing right now bro?" asked Joey.

"Shit. Was prolly going to twist up an L. Wanna watch me smoke? Maybe even get some second hand smoke in ya?"

"I don't want to smoke, but I can hang out for a bit," said Joey.

"Fine. Cool. You remember where I live?"

"Yeah, man. Be there in ten minutes."

"'right. See you soon," said Tyson.

Joey hung up and turned up the radio, as he headed to Tyson's house. One of his favorite new alternative rock groups, The High Beams, were playing their new single "Jungle Above.'" Joey couldn't help but jam out in his car, making many heads turn driving by, but he couldn't care less. He tried singing the words out loud without botching every line. After he forgot a few lines, he stopped in embarrassment, even though he was by himself.

He pulled up to the house Tyson shared with three other roommates, two of which sold weed. Tyson, on the other hand, was going to school at a nearby community college and helped his Dad at his auto shop a few times a week for a little extra cash. Tyson was actually a bright kid, but typically he hid his intelligence when he hung out with Joey and the rest of their friends.

Joey walked up to the front door and knocked twice. He could hear the door being unlocked. Tyson's roommate, Big Steve, opened the door and greeted Joey with a blank stare. "You Tyson's boy, right?"

"Yes," said Joey, as he hovered in the shadow of Tyson's large roommate.

A cloud of smoke made its way through the door before he pulled Joey inside.

"Don't need the neighbors smelling this super dank dank," said Big Steve. "Tyyyyyy!" he yelled.

"Wasssssup?" Tyson shouted back from the other room.

"Your boy," Big Steve stopped to look at Joey. "Joey," he continued.

"Joey is here!" shrieked Tyson.

"Why didn't you tell me we were having company?" asked Big Steve.

"Shut your fat ass up and bring him in here," said Tyson.

Joey entered the kitchen where Tyson and his other roommates were hanging out, passing cigars full of marijuana back and forth. The room was so smoky that it looked like there was a fog machine plugged in somewhere. It made Joey cough a bit.

"Ah, see I told you you'd get some contact high in ya," said Tyson, as he got up to greet Joey with dap.

"I can barely breathe in here," said Joey, as the marijuana smoke entered his body through his mouth and nose.

"You'll feel much better in a little bit, man," said Tyson, as he took a big drag from one of the large thick blunts going around.

"Oh, I'm sure," Joey said, sarcastically.

"Take a seat, my light-skinned brotha," said Tyson, as he pulled up a chair.

"So Tyson," said Joey. "How the hell can I come up with some money, my friend?"

"Well, that's a very good question. There are many ways..."

Tyson took another large hit from the marijuana-filled cigar.

"Dude, I always see you with money. You must have some good ideas," said Joey, as the smoke went into his eyes, causing them to burn for just a moment.

"There are legal ways. And then there are easy ways. As well as moral ways and immoral ways," said Tyson.

"What do you mean?"

Tyson exhaled a large cloud of haze. "Have you thought about selling chronic? I could prolly hook you up with Big Steve if you think you can move some bud."

He passed the blunt to his other roommate they all called JJ.

"Nah, man, I'm not good with all that," said Joey.

"All right, all right. I should have figured."

"Yeah, man. Let's think of other ideas first," said Joey, laughing, as the marijuana started to hit him from all of the second-hand smoke lingering around him.

"Maybe I can put you on the block and sell yourself to these ratchets. You got good dick to sell?" asked Tyson before he started laughing.

"C'mon man, I'm serious," said Joey, as he laughed with his friend.

"Okay, Ummm" said Tyson before he put his hand on his chin and began to think to himself.

"I know you're a smart dude. You can come up with something," said Joey.

A smile appeared on Tyson's face, before he said, "I can't believe we haven't thought of this yet. Why don't you just ask your followers for money?"

"Huh?" said Joey.

"Yeah, man. You got like what forty million followers on FaceSpace, don't you? With that God page?"

"Forty eight million, but yeah around there."

"Exactly. All you have to do is ask. People give money to churches, charities, stuff like that. I don't think your page would be any different. Haven't you noticed everytime you say something to these people they listen, and then do whatever you say? I know it isn't the most righteous way, but it may be the easiest right now," said Tyson.

"I think you're right. Maybe I should do that. But how?"

"I don't know. Aren't there like websites you can set up for donations or something? I think there's one called gofundus.com or something."

"Never heard of it."

"Wait no. It's called fundmeplease.com. Yeah, a lot of people use it for causes, organizations, various donations, even companies use it to get start up cash and what not. I think that's your best bet," said Tyson.

"I knew you would be able to help me out," said Joey.

"That's what I do, Bruh Bruh."

Joey pulled out his cell phone and opened up his Findoo app. He searched for the website for FundMePlease, and found it almost instantly. He clicked it and opened it up. Joey read all the rules and regulations, then checked out some of the other campaigns. He saw all sorts of different types of fundraisers, many by people that needed money for hospital bills, disabled veterans, some non-profit organizations, as well as people trying to get money for all sorts of projects, from funding someone's bachelor party or aiding fire victims to replacing a young boy's hearing aids to covering the costs of a celebration for a bullying victim.

Joey wanted to make sure he put his campaign in the correct category, and did it all by the book, so he wouldn't get in trouble later. He researched it for almost an hour while Tyson and his roommates continued to roll up their favorite plant, and smoke it non-stop throughout the night.

This was nothing new to them, but Joey didn't typically sit in a room full of marijuana. Needless to say, he got his very own contact high just from breathing.

"How's it going over there, Joe?" asked Tyson.

"This is freaking awesome. 'Bout to start my campaign right now!"

"Sweet man. I wish you luck. Also, don't forget who gave you the idea. Your boy Tyson."

Tyson took a puff of the joint he had just rolled.

"You know I won't," said Joey, as he went back to his phone. He finally clicked on the button, 'Start Campaign' and filled in all of the information.

He created an organization that he called the Internet God Foundation and filled out all the fields required before writing up a lengthy description of what his organization was all about. He claimed that the money raised from the fundraiser would be put towards Internet research about God, and all forms and types of religion, with no bias or prejudice against any one type of person or religion.

Joey also claimed that twenty percent of the funds raised would also be donated to various churches and other religious organizations and other non-profit associations that needed help across the country and even internationally including in Mexico, Italy, Japan, Ghana, Germany, France, China, Vietnam, Korea, to name a few. Joey had no plans to actually use the money for that reason, but he felt he had to say what he needed to get the money.

He then came to the section that asked him for the amount he hoped to raise, and for how long the fundraiser would last.

He first entered in "$50,000" before he realized that wasn't enough money. He thought long and hard about how much he would need. He looked underneath at a disclaimer that read: "If your goal is not reached, fundmeplease will take 10 percent of all donations." Then it said, "If your goal is reached, fundmeplease will take just four percent of all donations."

Sweet. So I get to keep the money no matter what. Joey started to enter a new amount —$7,000,000.00—in the column.

After that answer, it asked how long someone wanted to run the campaign. Although most of the campaigns he read about ran for thirty days, Joey wrote "One week" with a bold sense of confidence that his followers would react fast to his fundraiser.

Joey finished filling out all of the fields and clicked "*Submit Campaign.*"

A screen popped up that said, "An e-mail will be sent within 12-to-48 hours determining the status of your campaign. Good luck."

"I'm done."

Joey stood up from the chair in the haze-filled room.

"You got it taken care of already?" asked Tyson.

"Yes, man," he said. "Thanks again for the great idea. I owe you one."

"No problem, man. That's what friends are for," said Tyson, as he high fived Joey.

"I gotta run. I'm getting pretty tired. I'll hit you up tomorrow or something," said Joey.

"No doubt, bro. Have a good night," said Tyson, as he took a hit from a joint that had now become a tiny roach. Tyson burned his finger on the hot ember from the joint. "Ahhhh fuck."

"Be careful, dude. Don't burn the house down," said Joey, as he got up and headed to the front door.

"Oh, you know we're not gon' be burning the house down," said Tyson in this goofy voice he did when he got really high.

"Later, broham," said Joey, as he opened the front door and left the smoke-filled room.

The next afternoon, Joey woke up from a plethora of wild dreams he had throughout the night. He finally opened his eyes and looked at his alarm clock, which read 12:45. He got up and went to the bathroom with a bad case of morning wood.

When Joey got out of the bathroom, he sat down at his computer desk, and turned on his computer. It booted up, and he clicked on the Internet button. He logged into his PMail account and, to his surprise, he had already received an e-mail back from an automated response at fundmeplease.com. The e-mail read:

> "Congratulations! Your campaign was approved.
> See it here at
>
> www.fundmeplease.com/entry/godisgood/campaign3
> 37474939287

"Yessssss!" Joey yelled, as he sat in his room in nothing but boxers. He then opened up the URL search tool bar and typed in FaceSpace.com. It automatically logged him into his page for God.

He went back to the e-mail he had just received and copied it with his mouse. He went to his God page and clicked on '*Write Post*' and began to type.

> To all of my loyal followers. We need your help. Anything you can give for your Lord and savior. We need you to send some money to people that need it.
>
> Please donate to us here:
>
> www.fundmeplease.com/entry/godisgood/campaign3 37474939287.
>
> God Loves You All"

Joey finished typing so he then clicked on *Publish Post*. And, in instant, the post went live and all of God's followers began to flock to his newest post calling on them all to donate to his crowdfunding campaign.

As Tyson predicted, within moments, the word got out, and Joey's followers started giving.

The response was much larger than Joey could have ever anticipated. He sat back and watched it all unfold as his campaign began to grow larger and larger with every like, share, and comment that people left.

Joey decided not to write any more posts that week. He wanted to make sure that donating to his fundraising campaign had the highest possible reach among his 48 million followers, and growing. He also tried to keep himself off the radar and the grid while the days went by so nobody tried to intercept his campaign.

About a week later, Tyson heard a knock on his door. Big Steve answered it. He looked at Joey with a small grin and yelled out, "Hey Tyyyy, your boyfriend is back!"

Joey walked into the room with his hands in the pockets of his sweatshirt.

"What's going on!?" asked Tyson, as he took a big rip from his three foot bong. He started coughing like a mad man, before exhaling the potent marijuana smoke from the bong.

"It worked, bro," said Joey with a huge smile.

"What worked?" Tyson continued to cough because the weed was too strong and he took it through a three-foot bong.

"The campaign? Fundmeplease? I just got the money transferred into my account, bro!"

"Oh, yeah. How did that go, bro?" Tyson began to pack the bowl to the bong with more weed. You tell me."

Joey pulled his hands out of his pockets holding two huge stacks of hundred dollar bills, one stack in each hand, before he tossed it over to his wild friend.

"Holy smokes!"

Tyson took a break from the bong and stared at the money that Joey had just tossed him.

"This is real?" asked Tyson, as he started to smell the stacks of cash.

"Yepppp."

"How much did you end up getting?"

"Five," said Joey, as the smoke from Tyson's bong rose around him. He held his breath and turned his head away from it.

"Five? Five what? Five hundred? Five thousand? Five what?" asked Tyson, as he walked over to Joey and began to hug him.

"Five Million. Five million dollars," said Joey, with the emphasis on million, as Tyson's face lit up like he had seen a ghost. A rich ghost.

"Fii....fa...fiiiv.....five million?????" asked an astonished Tyson.

"Well, five point six and some change, I guess, to be more exact," said Joey.

"You're fucking kidding me, right, bro?" asked Tyson.

"Na, man. And that's fifty grand right there for you. There's more to come, but I just wanted to give you a little something for helping me get started you know," said Joey.

"Yeah, man, this is cool for now," said Tyson, as he began to laugh and count the fresh hundred dollar bills in his hands.

"I gotta run. We have a lot to discuss though," said Joey, as he headed for the door.

"Anything you need, King, God. Champ. Whatever you want me to call you, you rich ass motherfucker!"

"Maybe we can go out and have a good night tomorrow or something. It's on me," said Joey.

"Sounds like a fuckin plan!" said Tyson.

"Oh wait. It's Tuesday tomorrow. Nothing happens on a Tuesday," said Joey.

"Bro, when you're rich as fuck...every day is Friday, my G."

"Certainly, man. I'll see you tomorrow. Get the boys together. Oh, and no Oscar. Fuck him."

Joey walked out the door.

"Sure! No Oscar! No problem!" said Tyson, but Joey had already left the room.

Before Joey got back into his car, he pulled out his phone and opened up his FaceSpace App.

He clicked on '*Write Post*' and started to type...

I never wanted power, but now that I have it, it feels like the shit.

I never wanted to be the shit, until I realized its endless

possibilities.

Joey hit '*Publish Post*', and then he started to giggle before he opened up his car door. He got into his car, started it, and headed straight to the new car dealership down the street. He had some money to spend.

Chapter Sixteen
The Book of Riches

SINCE JOEY'S CAMPAIGN HAD ENDED and his checking account had more zeros in it than Joey ever thought he could make in his whole lifetime, his first thought was to head over to the new car lot and purchase a new automobile. He was amazed at how much more fun it was to shop for a car when he actually had enough money to pay for it in his pocket. No worries about getting a car loan or even a used car that hopefully didn't have the pedometer manipulated.

It just took him ten minutes of walking around the lot to pick out a candy-red Burrarri with custom rims and a custom engine. He could have gotten the same car in white or blue but that would have required ordering it and a one month wait time. Joey wanted his new car now. He was determined to drive it out of the dealership.

His beautiful new two-door sports car went 215 miles per hour, and 0-to-60 in 2.4 seconds. He spent $120,800 on his new car, paid for in cash, but he didn't stop there. He went directly from the dealership to the mall so he could go on a shopping spree.

In just two hours, he went into no fewer than ten stores, only stopping to buy the clothes he wanted. He purchased everything he ever dreamed of, from designer shirts at $175 a shirt, to a $450 sports jacket, and then he went to the consumer electronics store where he purchased a 72-inch 3D flat screen television with ultra-high definition that cost almost six thousand dollars.

On the way home, he stopped at the supermarket where he usually couldn't buy more than $20 worth of groceries at a time. But today, he was able to give the clerk hundreds of dollars in cash for all the groceries he bought for his family and himself. She hadn't had a cash order like that in a long time and checked out the authenticity of the $20 and $50 bills. But Joey wasn't bothered by that.

Later that day, he even began searching on the Internet for some information about a place of his own that he could move into. He decided he'd rent a place near his parents' home until he figured out where he wanted to permanently live or move to.

Later that night, Joey made plans to meet up with Tyson, Henry, and Chris to take them all on a trip to Atlantic City. Joey told them that he was treating them all to dinner as well as getting the best seats at any of the top shows in town. They'd even spend a little time at the casinos to gamble a bit. Tyson could use some of his $50,000 but Joey would give Henry and Chris $2,000 each so they could enjoy some gambling too.

Joey was definitely prepared to indulge himself and his friends and to spend some more of the money his followers had provided him with. After all, he still had close to $5 million left. He had never been so appreciative of his followers until now.

Joey pulled out his phone, dialed Tyson, and put it on speakerphone as he drove home in his new car full of the essentials and additional random stuff he had purchased throughout the day.

Tyson answered after a few rings. "Joeyyyyy!!!! My favorite person in the world! You pumped for tonight?" asked Tyson.

"Hell yeah, man! Aren't you? You sure sound like it," Joey said.

"Of course, Joseph! This is the first time you're taking all of us out. With the exception of Oscar, of course. Have you thought twice about maybe inviting him to come along with us? You guys have been besties for like forever," said Tyson.

"Hell no, man. He did me dirt and now that I'm doing good...

I hope he's jealous. I would have never fucked his girlfriend. That was just wrong and I can't forgive him. Sorry man."

"Okay, okay. I got you. No Oscar, that's fine. The boys said they'll be ready by six to head out. I think Chris has to work until four or five. I forget."

"Positively, man. Sounds good!"

"I wanted to say thanks again for this money, Joey. Now I can pay off all my student loans and go out and get messed up with my boys!"

"No problem, pal. And don't worry about tonight. It's all on me. I got it. Unless of course you want to use some of your money at the casino. If not, I'll give you some more money."

"Look at Mister Big Baller over here. Okay, well then, I will see you later."

"See ya later, broooo."

"Don't forget to wear your best cologne. We going to get some BISHES tonight!"

The call ended as Joey heard Tyson's bong beginning to bubble in the background just before the call dropped.

"That wild bastard," Joey said to himself, as he drove back home.

* * *

Over in New York City, at the I.S.I. headquarters, Special Agent Kenny Owens had been driving himself crazy trying to find new leads on the God page case he had been working on around the clock. He searched the Internet on Findoo for anything he could discover but the only thing anybody could say about the page was that it had been inactive for four years until recently when the page had made its first post.

As Kenny searched, he listened to his favorite song, "Where the Wind Rolls" by his favorite country singer, Billy Brooks.

"I'm going to get you, kid or man or whoever you are. Just wait. You're gonna slip up, and I'm going to be right there to catch you," agent Owens said, as he took a large sip of coffee. He looked as if he was in some sort of sadistic trance as his computer screen reflected off of his brown eyes.

Later that night, Joey and his friends rode in the back of a stretch limousine filled with champagne, wine, bottles of vodka, whiskey, gin, rum, and ice cold beers in a fridge nestled in between the seats. The limo was on its way to Atlantic City where the boys planned to paint the city red. Joey took it upon himself to stick his body out of the sun roof window, smoking a Cuban cigar and throwing his hands in the air, as he screamed at the top of his lungs, "This is

AWESOME!!"

Joey felt his lower body start to vibrate before he dropped down to the inside of the limo to look at his phone. He had received a text from Laura that read:

> Have fun tonight Joe. Hope to see you soon, you gorgeous, handsome man

Joey began to text back as his friends made a ruckus in the back of the stretch limo, passing bottles around, laughing, and having fun.

Joey texted back.

> "I miss you Laur... "

Chris stood up, bent over in the limo, and popped open a bottle of champagne and shouted: "Here's to our boy Joey Da Gawdd."

The other guys picked up glasses, as Chris began to pour very high class and expensive champagne into his friends' glasses, spilling it everywhere.

After a couple of toast, Joey opened up his FaceSpace app to write a new post for his followers to read, not realizing he was becoming more tipsy by the minute.

Joey began to type:

> The question is, "Do you want me to be an honest
> God? Or do you want me to be a fun God? or
> do you want me to be a righteous God? Or
> do you want me to be a wrong God?

Joey clicked the *'Publish Post'* button. He then raised his empty champagne glass and shouted to Chris, "Fill me up, brother!!!"

The boys stumbled out of the stretch limousine and headed next to the Lone Star casino, which also housed a worldwide-known steakhouse that specialized in T-bones and lobster. They arrived at Lone Star reeking of liquor, booze, and all different kinds of cologne. The crew had all dressed in suits and tuxedos, ready to have an unforgettable night.

Throughout the night, one thing that was consistent was that money was continually being spent, and bottles were being popped, as the crew got drunker than they even knew was possible.

After an amazing dinner with fabulous food, the group moved onto the next casino, Atlantic City Casino, trying their luck at craps, roulette, blackjack, and some Texas Hold'Em. After a couple of hours of betting, some of the boys were up, and some were down. But it didn't matter because Joey kept giving them spending cash for the night, as much as twenty thousand each. He didn't care about money any more now that he had millions. He just wanted to impress his friends with his new fortune.

After going to at least three different casinos, Joey, Tyson, Chris, and Henry made their way to the best nightclub in town, called Rain, which had a fifty dollar cover charge. Joey had Tyson arrange for them to be on the guest list so the crew did not have to pay to get in. That was because Joey had paid for a two thousand dollar V.I.P. table that came with numerous bottles, chasers, sitting space, and access into the millionaire's gentlemen's club next door, featuring the hottest strippers in New Jersey. But the boys decided they'd take their shot at the night club with real, normal women before they'd called it quits and head over to the strip club.

Girls flocked to the crew at their V.I.P. table because most of the women that went there knew that only rich folks could afford to get a V.I.P. table at Rain. Stunning women from all around the Tri-State area, as well as the rest of the world, came up to Joey, Tyson, Henry, and Chris, throwing themselves at the young men. Tyson was ecstatic all night, making out with several beautiful women and dancing with the hottest ones.

Joey met one pretty girl who called herself Rosa. They danced throughout the night, but Joey could not stop thinking about

Laura. He was just concerned with having a good time with his friends, as they continued to dance the night away.

Bottle after bottle, cigar after cigar; the boys partied harder and harder. Chris ended up trying to break-dance battle with another guy on the dance floor. It seemed everybody was cracking up all night. Joey even started to bust out some moves with women everywhere. The crew were having the time of their lives.

Around two a.m., after bouncing back and forth from dinner clubs to casinos to night clubs, the crew finally ended up at the gentleman's club, some of them somewhat drunker than the others. Tyson was stumbling on the sidewalk, as Henry and Chris tried to hold him up before entering the sleazy stripper private club.

They walked in and flashed their I.D.s to the 6'6, 350+ pound security guard at the front door. Joey paid fifty dollars each, so all of his friends could get inside. He even tipped the guard a hundred dollars on top of the cover.

Joey and the boys walked in and sat in the front row by the stage that contained four different poles, with two striking, luscious ladies swinging around. They were shaking their stuff to a new song with the bass vibrating from their butt cheeks.

Tyson stood up and said, "We are in heaven, boys!!" His friends stood up and cheered with him. The other tourists in the club looked over at the group like they were insane.

Chris, the only one who actually won any money at one of the casinos from playing craps, started to make it rain singles as a good-looking Latina lady bounced her booty up and down on the stage. The DJ announced that the voluptuous Latin dancer's name was "Felina" and the boys stared in awe as she performed on stage doing what she did best.

After about half an hour of throwing money at Atlantic City's finest strippers, getting a few lap dances, and having a great time, Chris stood up and walked over to the bar. There, he ordered a few more beers for his group before noticing someone interesting to the right at the end of the bar. Chris grabbed his beers and carried them back to the group sitting at the front of the stage.

"Yo guys," said Chris as he placed the beers on the table, pressed up against the stage.

"What's poppin?" asked Henry over the loudness of the music and other people talking.

"Y'all know that country singer, Bobby Brooks or something?" asked Chris to his friends.

"Ummm, I don't listen to country, but I've heard of him," said Henry.

"Wait a second, where's Joey?" asked Chris.

"He just got up to get his own lap dance," said an extremely wasted Tyson, who could barely keep his eyes open.

"Oh snap. I think he knows that guy, Bobby Brooks," said Chris.

"Billy Brooks," said Tyson. "His name is Billy Brooks. My dad loves him for some reason."

About forty yards away, Joey was just finishing up his lap dance with a stripper named "Saphire" in the private room. Joey tipped her a hundred dollars, a minute into his lap dance, spraying fives and tens all over the young lady. Saphire went in to kiss Joey after he took a swig of his bottle of beer. She made out with him and moved a pill from the back of her tongue onto his. He swallowed it before he realized what had happened.

"What was that?"

"Some Ecstasy, cutie," said the red-headed stripper.

"Oh, shit," said Joey, as the pill began down his esophagus.

Within a few moments, he knew it would start digesting through his stomach as it slowly went into his bloodstream.

"Now, enjoy this baby and then buy another lap dance in an hour from me," said Saphire, as she continued to grind on Joey as she pushed her breasts up into his face.

The lap dance came to an end when Saphire walked Joey back

out to his friends and he sat down with them.

"That was really intense," said Joey, as his friends threw tens, fives, and ones on the stage for a pretty big-butted dark woman they announced as "Monique."

"It was really that good, huh?" asked Henry.

"Yeah, bro, Saphire was amazing," said Joey, as he watched his favorite new stripper walking away and waving goodbye.

"Yo Joey, I'm glad you're out here. Look over at the bar over there. Isn't that the country singer dude, Billy Brooks?" asked Chris.

Joey squinted his eyes as the Ecstasy, also known as Molly, began to kick in faster than he could have imagined it would. He took a sip from the bottle of beer he had and stared a bit longer.

"Yeah, I think that's him," said Joey.

"That's pretty cool," said Tyson. "Why don't we go over to him and say, 'What's up?'"

"You sure you want to do that?" asked Henry, as he took a ten-dollar bill and put it inside the thong that 'Monique' was wearing.

"Thank you, baby," said the big-booty stripper.

"Let's go see if we can get a photo with him," said Joey. "That would be hilarious," he continued. "You can post it on FaceSpace later. Just don't tag me," Joey laughed while he rallied his friends.

"Fuck it, let's do it," said Tyson, as he stood up and followed Joey and the other boys to the bar.

They walked up to the country singer, who was with an entourage of friends and fans surrounded by strippers talking to him and taking pictures with him.

"Hey, Mr. Brooks," said Joey.

"What's up?" asked Tyson.

The country star looked over at the group of silly drunken buffoons. He ignored them for a moment and continued talking to one of the striking strippers who was talking to him.

"Hello," said Joey, finally getting the singer's attention.

"How can I help you, boys? Can't you see I'm trying to have a good time with my people?" said Billy Brooks.

"Me and my friends were just trying to say 'Hi' and wanted to get a picture with you or something. Maybe an autograph," said Joey as he went in to shake the country star's hand.

"I don't have time for this," said Brooks as he left Joey hanging for his handshake.

"Wow," said Joey.

"Just let it go, man," said Chris.

"Nah man, this motherfucker thinks he's too good for us. Fuck that!" said Joey.

"Boy, you better get to stepping," said Billy Brooks in an irate tone.

"Or what?" said Joey, as he shoved the country star.

At that moment, Brooks' entourage jumped up and grabbed Joey.

"You want something, asshole?" asked Billy Brooks before he swung at Joey.

Joey ducked and punched Brooks once in the stomach, then, with a left hook to his face, the country star dropped to the floor.

The country star's friends and fans jumped onto Joey and started hitting him all over. Tyson then jumped to the call-of-action, and he started brawling with the country star's entourage. A big fight ensued in the gentleman's club before the security guards separated the two groups. They ended up kicking Joey and his friends out of the club.

While they were throwing the crew out, Joey screamed out, "I am God!!!!!!!!" and "Let me go!!! I am God."

The security guards, figuring they had a nut case on their hands, shook their heads and threw Joey out on his butt with his friends next to him.

Once outside, they laughed it off and ran down the street, high fiving each other.

"That was fucking nuts!" said Tyson.

"We're lucky they didn't throw us in jail!" said Henry.

"Our Joey just punched big shot country music legend Billy Brooks in the damned face!" said Chris.

"That was crazy," said Joey who had a few bruises on his face from getting hit by Mr. Brooks' accomplices.

The crew kept running like a pack of wild animals up to the stretch limo Joey had rented out for the night.

"Crazy ass night," said Henry as he opened up the door and they all got into the limo.

"You might want to get out of here quick," said Chris to the limo drive.

"What happened?" asked the limo driver.

"We're not paying you to ask questions! Just drive, man!" said Joey as the Ecstasy hit him in full effect. He pulled out his cell phone and opened up his FaceSpace app.

He clicked on the 'Write Post' button and began to type:

> To all my beloved followers,
> Boycott Billy Brooks!
> This man is the devil. Do not listen to his music or support this man! Plus it sucks crap!
> #BoycottBillyBrooks!

Joey clicked '*Publish Post*' and then sat back with his friends as he began rolling harder and harder.

"Tonight was fucking epic," said Joey.

"Hell yes!" said Tyson, as he sprawled across the seat in the back and closed his eyes, while smiling and still laughing with his friends.

"We'll remember this forever," said Henry.

Chapter Seventeen
The Book of God

IT WAS A DAY LATER, and Special Agent Kenny Owens was attempting to take a break from his job. Owens, a humungous Billy Brooks fan, followed his Tweeker account religiously. He would receive Billy Brooks' 'Tweeks' regularly. Like most celebrities, Brooks 'tweeked' to stay in touch with his fans by writing messages that had to be 160 characters or less.

Owens was excited to see his favorite country star had posted a new Tweek and immediately opened up the musician's page to find out the update. Billy Brooks' newest Tweek read, "Howdy y'all! I've been doing music for years now. I have millions of fans but I must tell you all something. First of all, I'm a man of God."

Reaching close to the maximum of 160 characters, Brooks wrote his second Tweek, a continuation of his first one:

"I believe in God with everything in me, first and foremost. I don't know if you have been on FaceSpace yet..."

Tweek #3 –"but he's told me and the WORLD that I should stop making music. I've already contacted my agent and all of my future tour show dates have been cancelled..."

Tweek #4 –"Anyone who's pre-ordered tickets will get a refund. But this is opening a door to my future goals. I will now look to open up my new business venture, Ho-Down."

Tweek #5 –"It's a country food Buffet/Restaurant. I'm sorry for any inconvenience, but I'm not sorry for doing God's will. Your humble servant, Billy Brooks".

Owens crushed his O-Daisy's cup that was almost full to the top with Ray's Cola out of pure anger.

"What?" Owens screamed.

He had purchased second row tickets to Brooks' upcoming show in New York City a week away.

Without washing the soda pop off of his hands, he angrily opened up FaceSpace on his cell phone, and searched for the God page. Owens opened it up and typed a comment on the recent post by God's page about country star Billy Brooks.

Posted at 3:29PM Aug. 28th

It read:

> Listen here....GOD! First of all, off the record...I
> don't know who you are or why you do the things that
> you do. I don't know why you do great things like ask
> people how they could change the world; and then
> turn around and do horrible things like sabotaging
> businesses and artists. You're ruining people's lives!!
> You are NOT GOD! You understand me!? NOT
> GOD! I don't care that my career is on the line,
> dealing with you you'll find a way to ruin it anyway,
> but rest assured, REST ASSURED I will find you, and
> I will bring you to justice. I will HUNT YOU
> DOWN!

The Special Agent's blood began to boil as he continued to type:

> You spread filth. You trick these people into
> believing in you by doing good things here and there!
> These idiots may buy your bullshit but I'm not, you get
> that boy? Yeah, didn't know I knew you were a male
> did you? I may not know exactly who you are, JOEY,
> but as you can see, I know your name and you're
> dealing with Special Agent Kenny Owens now.
> No more news reporters, no more app companies,

you're screwing with the big boys now. You use the Lord's name in vain? Blasphemously calling yourself God. Who do you think you are JOEY? You must be stopped. You WILL be stopped! You know what? I'm going to stop writing now because I'm already giving a piece of crap like you more attention than you deserve. But you'll be getting all the attention' you need behind bars. Believe in THAT!

Joey was notified of the comment the moment it popped up on his screen. The moment his phone made the distinct noise for FaceSpace, he checked it and read the comment. Joey laughed a bit, as Owens seemed to have been driven far too crazy. This entertained Joey, as he felt his power was now driving his adversary mad. However, even though he didn't know his full name, Special Agent Kenny Owens knew Joey's FIRST name. Joey knew this, and it had him thinking long and hard.

About ten minutes later, Joey's phone rang. "Hello?" Joey answered, as he put his ear to the cell phone.

"Hey, I'm about to get on the train. I'll be there in an hour almost exactly," said Laura.

"Thank God. I need you. Hurry up. God hurry up," said Joey.

"I know you need me. That is exactly why I'm coming. You really got us into some shit and I LOVE it. What an adventure!"

JEFF YAGER *AND* SKYE BYNES

exclaimed Laura.

"You're the only person in this world that could think this is cool. Laura, you're so effin' hot."

Joey started to laugh.

"Haha! I know. O.K., I'm on the train. I'll be there in a bit. I love you!"

"I love that you can hack."

"You're too funny! Bye!"

Laura hung up as she smiled. She loved the chase more than an easy grab.

Joey stayed seated as he breathed in and out. He grabbed his phone, and began to write a reply to Kenny's post.

Meanwhile, Special Agent Kenny Owens, whose obsession had brought him to the point of constantly checking to see if this Joey guy had answered or not, thought to himself, *This Joey's going down. I need to do something about this.*

He opened up a FaceSpace page called, Cyber Intellects Unite!, and began to write a post:

> Hey everyone, there's a big job offered to anyone who's willing to help me bring down a cyberterrorist. I'll need at least ten people. Help me out and make

some money! ONLY THE BEST. You will be deputized for this special assignment."

Owens formed a half-evil grin on his face. He was sure this would help him in his quest to nail this terrorist. He sat pondering, wondering what else he could do to take down this demon who called himself God. He then opened FaceSpace back up to check the comment again, and this time 'God' had replied to Agent Owens: His post read:

> I can't listen to you idiot, you're typing, ya big dummy.

This made Kenny even more upset after reading the childish answer Joey had written him.

"FUCK!" Owens screamed, as he flipped his desk over, computer and all. His breathing turned uneasy, as tears began to form in his eyes out of pure anger. He opened up his wallet and looked at the two worthless Billy Brooks concert tickets for next week, knowing he would not be able to see his favorite country star anymore. He grabbed his jacket and headed to headquarters.

Back at Joey's, someone was knocking on his door.

Joey saw his former best friend Oscar standing in the doorway.

"Dude, we need to ..."

"No, we don't," said Joey, interrupting Oscar before he could finish his sentence "Don't ever fucking come to my house again, and don't ever speak to me again. I'm fucking serious, you FUCKING cunt!"

Joey lifted his hands up in a fighting stance like he wanted to punch his ex-best friend.

"No dude, please, man, just LISTEN! Fuckin'-"

"Dude, just stop. Go the hell away before I knock you the fuck out." Joey tried to slam the door, but Oscar stopped it from closing.

"Listen to me Joey. I just..."

But Oscar got cut off again this time by Joey's quick fist to Oscar's mouth, knocking him down the short flight of stairs on Joey's porch. Oscar held his mouth, looking up at Joey in astonishment. Joey slammed his parent's front door and turned around.

He brought his hand to his mouth. *Man that hurts,* Joey thought. He then turned back around, opened the door and said, "Oscar, I'm sorry." But Oscar had already left. Disappointed, Joey closed the door and leaned up against it, before sliding down into a seated position on the floor.

Kenny Owens was driving his car, and couldn't help but scream things out loud to himself.

"Disrespectful BRAT! How DARE this kid or man, whoever this Joey is, disrespect me?! Eight years of college and graduate school for some idiot on FaceSpace to call ME an idiot!"

Owens' mind was racing at a million miles an hour. He had trouble concentrating on the road. Thankfully, it was clear with just a few people riding around as he drove his company- issued black cruiser.

Joey heard a knock on the door, thinking it was Oscar, he got up quickly and opened it, ready to apologize for hitting him in the face but it was Laura. Joey was in no way let down.

"Hey! Was anyone following you or anything?" Joey asked as Laura walked inside.

"I didn't really check. Our wall hasn't been hacked yet..."

"I meant, 'Did anyone follow you from the train station?'"

"No," said Laura. She continued, "And our definitions are still a step ahead so the second we get infiltrated, I'll know. Then and only then, we will need to worry. For now, and in the foreseeable future, your identity is a secret."

"Fair enough."

* * *

Special Agent Owens pulled up to the I.S.I. headquarters, parked his car, then took a minute to try and wind down. He got out of the car and headed inside. A few co-workers greeted him as he walked down the hall, looking for his direct boss, who was in his office. He'd never once had to go to his boss before, but his partners didn't want to help him on what had become a personal vendetta. This wasn't an assignment given to him, and most likely, there were others who tried and failed at finding Joey already.

Owens found his boss's office and knocked on the door before he heard, "Go ahead and come on in".

"Sir, there's this page," Owens said to Captain Fernly before he was cut off.

"Yes, on FaceSpace. You do understand that everything you wrote on there could be used against us," said the Captain. "You do know that no matter how wrong this Joey guy is, he could counter sue us for not having a warrant? You could shut this whole place down going rogue like you did!"

"But sir, this guy ..."

"I don't care!" Captain Fernly screamed back. "We could all lose our jobs over this mess. Stop worrying about everyone else and just do your job, Owens! Well actually, it was your job!" the

Captain said, flailing his arms in the air. "As much as I hate to have to do this, to protect the agency it's a necessary step."

"What do you mean?"

"You're fired! Yes, you're fired, Owens. Turn in your ID, your badge, and your gun. I never want to see your face around here again."

"Are you fucking kidding me?"

Owens shouted so loud that his co-workers could all hear him from outside of the captain's office.

"I gave years of my life to this place!" shouted Owens. "The one time I decide that I care about a particular case, I get fired for it? This is complete and utter nonsensical, nonsense and bull fucking shit."

Owens' kicked over the captain's computer table, causing the computer to crash to the floor.

When Owens suddenly realized what he had done, out of pure fear, he left the captain's office, and bolted out the door. He quickly walked over to the software room and stole six different discs for his cyber-vigilante mission. He then headed out of the building while stuffing them into his jacket as two security guards were suddenly in hot pursuit. But Owens had enough of a head start, and he was fast enough on his feet, that he was able to lose them after a couple of blocks.

Feeling like he was finally in the clear, Owens looked around to make sure he wasn't spotted as he ran to his car. He could still hear the captain screaming, "You're going to pay for that, Owens!"

He got into his car and sped off.

Joey popped open a can of Mountain Mist, and before taking a sip, said to Laura, "So do you know when the next Ralph n' Doug: The Critic Files episode comes on? It's supposed to be their first live episode on ViewTube special. I'm super excited."

"In literally three minutes," said Laura. "My ViewTube is always advertising it. They are easily the biggest ViewTube sensation on earth right now. I don't really watch them much anymore. I liked it better when they were doing the nostalgic-style stuff. Too many new movies now, in my opinion."

"I liked the older ones too, but there's a bunch of new movies that I've seen and still get a good kick out of it," said Joey, taking another sip and then burping right after.

"I'm opening the link," Joey continued. "You should watch it with me."

"I'll watch anything with you," said Laura. "You could make anything fun, I swear."

. . .

When former special agent Kenny Owens got home, he found everything knocked on the floor. *Good job, Kenny; let's just ruin everything.*

He began picking up his mess. His computer screen was cracked and now discolored, but not damaged enough to where he couldn't work on it. He went on to FaceSpace and to the CIU page to see if anyone had taken any offers. He was happy to see that quite a few people had answered his request. More than half of the applicants had gone to college for many years to perfect their craft. One even had a law degree.

He contacted six of the applicants: Janet Reilly, Marcus Oliver, Clifford Hendrix, Stanley Dunkin, Macy Burnham, and Felix Harper. Janet hadn't gone to college, but she seemed to have a hell of a resume, and, unknown to Kenny, had her own popular ViewTube show on hacking and computer repair named 'Hack n' Patch'. They were all more than willing to take the job, and Owens had some savings put aside, so he let them know that each were going to be paid according to what Kenny believed they were worth and how much work they could get done.

The one Owens determined would be getting paid the least was receiving seven thousand dollars for this special assignment, so it wasn't accurate to believe they were all going to be paid handsomely.

The six new hires were scheduled to meet Owens in the next few days, all travel paid. Owens had money saved up from his twenty years with the I.S.I., and he decided to take it upon himself to pay them so he could get the job done that had been driving him insane and that had even cost him his job. He. Of course, didn't mention to any of the new hires that he was no longer an employee of the I.S.I. and that this was a rogue or freelance assignment that he had decided to pursue on his own

During the next few days, as Owens was drilling his team on how to figure out who this "Joey" was and, once they figured that out, what to do with that information, Joey and Laura stayed by each other's side waiting for the shit to hit the fan.

Laura found that she was growing more tired by the day. She now had to keep up with Joey's God page, updating it every few hours due to the amount of infiltrations they were catching on every older firewall definition she had set up. She knew it would only be a matter of time before her software froze, even for a second, and they'd be caught.

Joey had given her a generous amount of money out of the five million that he had raised, so money wasn't the issue. Laura didn't relish the idea of somehow being pulled into Joey's hoax and possibly getting arrested, sent to jail or, almost as bad, having the anti-hacking business she had spent the last five years building up destroyed. Even if only one of her clients got hacked, or had his or her identity revealed, no one else would ever hire her again. Laura promised each and every client complete anonymity, and if someone figured out who Joey was, she could no longer make that promise or give that guarantee.

"These people don't give up," said Laura. "They're a second behind me at all times but damn, they're persistent. Let's just hope they don't notice the pattern that my software creates. Want to see an animation of them chasing us on the grid? It's pretty wild."

"No, it's OK." Joey was playing a game of Pissed off Penguins. "I'm finally about to beat stage 20 though, long enough wait, I'd say." But just then Joey ran out of turns. "Shit!"

Laura looked over at him. "You are so careless about this. They're starting to gain on us, and you're in no way worried?"

"Oh, I'm worried, trust me. There's just no point in flipping out about it. The second your program tells us that we're in for it, then we're in for it. Like you told me before, right?"

"Yea but, I'm getting worried, Joey. I know what I said, but now it's getting real."

Joey, caring about how she felt, made a suggestion.

"Tell ya what. If things get too bad, get outta here. We should go to the ATM and get you some more money, just in case."

"I don't want to leave you with this alone, Joey. I want us both to be OK," Laura said with a slight frown on her face.

"I'll be fine," Joey said with the most serious expression he'd ever worn. "If you want to come with me, we'll be fine. If necessary, I'll charter a private jet and fly us out of the country to some place where they don't have an extradition agreement with the U.S."

"Let me think about it," Laura replied.

It was only a few days later, and Owens was with the group of hired hackers who'd been working diligently on tracking down Joey's page, when Janet jumped up.

"I found him," she said.

"Good. Where?" asked Kenny.

The next day, Joey went on to his 'God' page and decided to make a somewhat random but meaningful post.

> "Good people are hard to come by, and fake
> people are hard to avoid... Remember this all the days

of your life."

Posted at 6:30 p.m. September 2.

It was 1:30 a.m. in Johannesberg, South Africa, and a family was sleeping on chairs in their small home. Their cottage wasn't in the best shape, but they had each other. As they were huddled together in their one-room house, they were in on the floor, when suddenly, someone kicked in their door and before they knew it, guns were in their faces.

"What the hell?" said Marcus Paton, the assault team leader. As he looked around at the family, he realized they must have been tricked.

"We're sorry," he said, as he and his team backed out of the house.

"Shit," Janet said to Paton over the smart phone she was using to communicate with him from the U.S.

"I was a little skeptical that a random-ass cyberterrorist would be in South Africa but, then again, you never know, right? But we just kicked in the door on a defenseless family. They had a baby in there."

"I see that. Not our fault. Let's get back to work," said Paton. "Besides, Owens assured me that he'll make good to the family for any damages to their home."

Clifford chimed in, "Back to work? Yeah, we need to, but have a heart, man. That poor family in there didn't even know what you meant when you said 'Sorry.' You're in Africa, so…"

"We know where we are, numb-nuts," said Paton. "Let's go. I feel bad but, what the hell. Let's just go."

Paton led his team out of the cottage, leaving behind the traumatized family, as they all ran back towards a helicopter that was waiting to airlift them out.

Joey and Laura were once again in their intimate mood when Joey's phone rang and Amber's picture was on the screen. He quickly hopped off of Laura and answered the phone.

"Hello?"

"Dude! Tyson's dead!"

"Who is this? This isn't Amber."

"It's Oscar, man. Tyson's dead."

"Oscar?"

Joey could make out Oscar trying his best to hold off tears, but failing miserably.

"I'm sorry, dude," said Oscar. "I'm sorry I called on Amber's phone, but I had to so you'd pick up. I've been trying to tell you for days now, but you wouldn't pick up, and no one else will tell you but Tyson's fucking dead man."

There was a silence.

"Are you there, Joey?" asked Oscar in a somewhat agitated voice.

Slowly Joey asked, "What the hell happened?"

"The gambling, man. Somehow he started gambling again, and things spiraled out of control."

"What do you mean?"

"You know – I mean *knew* – Tyson, Joey. Once he started gambling, he couldn't stop. He was up for a while, but it seems he got down just as quickly, and he wound up owing some very bad people a lot of money, and when he couldn't pay them, they killed him."

Oscar broke down sobbing.

"Listen, Oscar, if this is some kind of a joke to get back at me for cutting off our friendship, you got me, bad. Yeah, you got me."

"This is no joke, Joey. Unfortunately, it's the truth."

"Man, this is just awful. I just don't understand it. Tyson knew I had a lot of money. He knew he could ask me for money if he was in a bad spot."

"Maybe he was too embarrassed to come to you for help?"

"Bull shit! That's what friends are for, Oscar. Friends don't screw their friends' girlfriends. Friends help their friends if they need money. Friends don't let their friends get killed over something stupid like money. It's only money, and if what you say is true, Tyson is dead because he couldn't pay off his gambling debts."

As he finished saying the last sentence, Joey suddenly realized that it was that night on the town in Atlantic City that probably got Tyson gambling again. But it was supposed to just be one night of celebrating, not the beginning of another round of destructive gambling for his good friend Tyson. They had been friends since forever.

Joey started to sob, as he realized he would never be able to talk to or hang out with Tyson ever again.

He finally hung up the phone. Joey then just stared at his cell phone, as Laura tried to kiss him, but Joey wasn't able to form words, or move. He was frozen-numb, devastated by Oscar's tragic news.

Chapter Eighteen
The Book of Pain

UNABLE TO CONNECT WITH JOEY, and feeling rejected and not even knowing why, Laura eventually left his house. Joey still couldn't believe what he had just heard from Oscar, and he wasn't prepared to share the news with Laura because it would make it too real. He sat at his computer desk and began to cry as his tears turned to sobs. Tears rolled down Joey's face, as he thought about what he could have done to at least try to save Tyson. He knew he was partially to blame because he gave him all that money and then took him on a gambling spree to Atlantic City.

He had no clue that Tyson would get himself into such a predicament. Joey had completely forgotten about Tyson's gambling problem, since he knew he was going to Gamblers Anonymous meetings and he was supposed to have his addiction in check. Joey knew intellectually that his friend was responsible for his own actions, but in his heart, Joey still felt a certain amount of blame for what had happened to his friend.

He went onto his computer with tears falling from his face, and typed into the URL box "facespace.com."

Joey then went back to the post he had made asking people what they would do the change the world. He began to reread every comment and the answers that his followers gave him. But this time, their answers made him think long and hard.

He started to tear up reading some of the comments. It suddenly occurred to him that he was being a real jerk about the power he had accumulated. He also realized how greedy he had been with the money he had raised from his followers through Fundmeplease. Had he really done anything useful with all that money? Did he really need that $450 sports jacket? Was gambling and strip joints the best way to spend his wealth?

He knew that some lottery winners went on spending sprees finding within a year or two they would go from poor to wealthy to having more debt than the millions they had won. He realized if he didn't do things differently with his contributions from his followers, he was on the same disastrous path, with a dead friend to mourn because of mishandled money.

Sad but determined, Joey began to think of a plan.

He also realized there was some truth in what Special Agent Owens had mentioned, that he had hurt a lot of people because of his own personal issues. Much like God himself, many people had had to suffer and cope with life because of something one or few people, connected with his God page, in some way, had done.

Man...this could get bad, very bad, Joey thought. *These people that believed in me made me what I am. I wouldn't have anything, no money, no page, nothing without them.*

"I have to do the right thing," Joey said to himself.

Maybe there's a way I could give back, Joey thought, as he considered long and hard about something good he could do now to help a lot of people.

After a few minutes, he figured that maybe a charity that he believed in would be the best way to go. He opened up his search bar and typed in 'charity.' Quite a few results popped up: autism causes, breast cancer causes, cerebral palsy causes, Alzheimer's causes, thousands upon thousands of causes. But Joey felt no personal connection to any. He wanted to help something he believed in. He wanted to feel like he was really making a difference.

JEFF YAGER *AND* SKYE BYNES

Heart disease. Joey's mind sparked as he began to type it in immediately. His mother's illness was due to heart disease, and Joey really felt in his heart that this was a good charity that he could help out with at least some of the money from his followers.

Joey walked downstairs and asked his parents if they had any envelopes and stamps. His mom had some of each and gave them to Joey. "Thanks," he said before running back upstairs.

When he got into his room, Joey pulled out a checkbook that he had received from his bank, and he started filling out different checks for various organizations. After writing a check for $250,000 to an organization that was fighting heart disease in women, Joey wrote another check for $250,000 to a local special needs children center. Then, he wrote checks for $100,000 each for ten different cancer research organizations, as well as for other diseases including HIV, fighting homelessness in America, starvation in Africa, and a dozen others.

He donated to one company that fed homeless children in other countries as well as an organization that helped feed hungry children in his country too. He wrote one check to the Camden school district for $1,000,000.

All of the checks ranged from $100,000 to $1,000,000. He wanted to give away most of the money he had left from his

271

fundmeplease.com campaign and put it to good use. He wanted to do something special. He saved a little bit for himself to put into a savings account for him to live on, but the majority of it was going to go to people that actually needed it even more than he did.

He decided to become the change in the world people needed to see. Joey felt like he had taken advantage of his new found power, and it wasn't right. Writing out those checks for worthy organizations made him feeling a sense of pride, calm, and purpose that he had never known before. It felt so much better than squandering the money on that night on the town.

Joey heard his phone ringing, before he saw it was Laura and answered it.

Before Laura could say anything, Joey blurted out, "Hey Laura, I'm really sorry."

"What's going on?"

"I'm not doing so great."

"I could see that. That's why I left. What's wrong?"

"My best friend, Tyson, was killed. I guess he got himself involved with a bet that he couldn't pay off. And they killed him. Can you believe it? You hear about these things in the news. You see it happening in the movies and on TV. But you don't expect it to happen to one of your closest friends. Tyson was part of my crew.

There were four of us."

"What happened?" Laura asked, astonished and saddened.

"It seems he couldn't pay a damned basketball bet that he lost, and he got fucking killed. And I can't stop thinking that it's all my fault."

"Oh my gosh. I'm so sorry, Joe."

"It's okay. It's not *your* fault," he said.

"And neither is it yours. You didn't force him to get himself into that mess. Yes, it's horrible, but you can't blame yourself."

"But I did give him a lot of money, and I took him to Atlantic City. I feel that if I didn't give him the money and if I hadn't taken him gambling, he never would have done it. Or even had the capability to do it, you know what I mean?"

"How were you supposed to know that's what he'd do with the money? Did you know he had such a bad gambling problem?"

"I knew he used to have one, but he told me he was in a support group for it, and he was okay with it. It isn't fair. It isn't right."

"Even if you knew he once had a gambling problem, you thought he was over it. Also, you can't take responsibility for what others do, especially when it comes to money."

"I wish I could agree with you."

Laura continued, trying to reassure Joey. "If there's anything I can do for you, you know I'm your girl."

"I know. Thanks, Laura. I just need some time to think and process everything that's happened."

"I'm here for you if you just want to talk or anything. You also, most of all, need to forgive yourself for what happened to your friend."

"Thanks. You might be proud of me about this.'

"What's that?" asked Laura.

"I'm writing a bunch of checks to different organizations and foundations that need the money more than I do."

"Really?" she said.

"Yeah," Joey responded.

"Like all of it?"

"Not all, but most of it. I will probably keep four or five hundred thousand. And I have one million stored away in savings, in case we have to flee or some shit. But I'm giving away millions. I don't need all of this money, all of this power. This shit gets you into trouble."

"Wow, well even though I would never do that, that's very humble of you, Joe. I'm proud of you."

"Maybe my karma will get better after this. Who knows?"

"Next time I see you, I'll give you a nice little gift, like a blowjob or something."

"Whoa. All right. If you insist. And I'm going to give you at least twenty thousand more as a bonus payment for continuing to keep my God page unhackable and my identity secret."

"Fair enough. But you still have to take me out to dinner and a movie. But there may be some fellatio in there somewhere."

"You're insane, but I love you."

"Wait. What?"

"I mean I love your sense of humor."

"You said you love me, Joey. Don't whimp out on me."

"Did I?"

"Yes, yes you did. And it was cute. Don't worry, Joey, I think I love you too."

"You're amazing."

"You are, too. Now cheer up. I can hear you crying through the phone. Pick yourself up. I'll see you soon, okay? We'll plan something out."

"That sounds good."

"Talk to you later, babe."

The call ended, as a smile appeared on Joey's face. He continued to write more checks to different foundations and organizations including a support group for those addicted to gambling that he discovered through his online research. Before putting each check into an envelope, he would write out the organization's address, but he included no return address, and no note. Just the checks in each one, with a stamp attached to it.

He piled up the dozens of anonymous donation letters as a thought occurred to him. *Who the hell was that kid that came up to me at the gas station that one day a few weeks ago?*

He walked over to his laundry basket and started digging into it, throwing his clothes all over the floor of his room. At the bottom of the laundry basket, he saw the mixtape he had received from the young boy at the gas station. Joey picked it up, took the CD out of the plastic case it was in, and put it in the CD drive on his computer.

As the music began to play, a bunch of gun shots went off in the intro of the mixtape, scaring Joey, before the rapper, MC Connor, started going off in the first track.

Joey sat in his chair and listened to the rap from beginning to end, and then he listened to it again and then a third time. He ignored every text message and phone call that came in, so he could continue to listen to the mix tape.

He couldn't stop listening to the deep, lyrical rap songs. When it ended, Joey was in daze. He was amazed at how good it was and was ashamed with himself for not giving the CD that the young rapped had generously given to him a chance sooner.

The youthful MC Connor impressed the hell out of Joey. His rap had a mix of all the best aspects a hip-hop project would want powerful, meaningful lyrics over great beats and production. He suddenly felt like he had to do something for MC Connor, but didn't know how to get in contact with him.

Joey then picked up the case to the mix and realized that right on the front of the case read facespace.com/mcconnor.

"Duhhh, I should have known he'd be on there."

Joey heard a knock on his bedroom door and before he screamed out "What!" like he typically would, he instead said, "Come in".

It was his sister, Jane. She had been listening to the music from outside the door.

"Who *is* that?" asked Jane, as she bobbed her head to MC Connor's song "Living Life,'" which had a very fast and compelling beat that anybody would grasp on to.

"This is a rapper named MC Connor," said Joey.

"I've never heard of him," Jane said.

"He's this young kid. I met him at the Letz gas station a few weeks ago. He was selling his CD, but he gave me one for free because at the time I didn't have the money to buy it."

"This is really good. Can you burn me a copy?"

"Yeah, but it's underground. I'm not sure if you like this type of stuff."

"It sounds sick. Just burn me one, okay?"

"Okay, I got you."

As his sister left his room and shut the door, Joey looked at the CD.

"Hmmmm. People will really like this kind of stuff."

Maybe I can do something that will get more people to listen to it, Joey thought, as he navigated FaceSpace, and searched for MC Connor.

He found his page, but it only had 265 likes/followers, and not many comments or posts.

He then searched for MC Connor's ViewTube page, and found a few music videos that he had posted. They all had between a hundred and five hundred views. Joey felt bad, because he knew how good the music actually was, and he couldn't figure out why it had so few views or likes.

Chapter Nineteen
The Book of Faith

JOEY AND LAURA WERE CUDDLING in Joey's bed, staring into each other's eyes, holding each other like they would never let the other go. He felt more in love with Laura than he had ever been with any of his previous girlfriends. He didn't think he could fall for someone so fast after he and Amber broke up. But Laura was different from any girl he had ever met, and he knew he had to do whatever he could to keep her.

They may not have met in a traditional way, but the two felt something for one another like it was meant to be. Joey, at twenty-six, had been through enough romantic relationships, and break ups, that he knew "the real thing" when it happened, and Laura was the real thing. And it felt right from the start.

Most of all, Laura loved Joey for himself, faults and all. But her love made Joey want to be a better person. He felt some of the anger he had festering inside him for so long dissipating.

As he stared into Laura's eyes, Joey heard the notification sound coming from his computer. He got up and looked at his screen to see a message on his FaceSpace page. He clicked on it to open it.

The message was from a high school student named Jerome Atkins, and it read:

> "Dear God/Joey/Whoever you are
>
> My name is Jerome. I have been following your "God" page closely since it became active over the last month or so. I would like to offer you the opportunity to be interviewed by me. I have a certified ViewTube channel in which I interview Internet celebrities to help them boost their views and followers.
>
> I know you don't need any more followers, but I felt like you might be interested in giving the world your perception of everything. Some people are totally against you and your page, and are trying to get rid of it. Others are calling you some sort of rebel savior.
>
> Please, if you are interested, I live in Queens, NYC and can come to wherever you are. It would be really cool as I for one am a big fan of what you have been doing, regardless of what other people are saying.

Please get back to me about this. It would be greatly appreciated.

Thank you for your time.

Hope to hear from you soon,

Jerome

"Whoa," said Joey.

"What happened?" asked Laura.

"This guy, Jerome, just messaged me, asking me if I would want him to interview me for his ViewTube interview channel."

"That's nuts. You're not going to do it, right?"

"I don't know yet. Maybe. I mean shit, why not? Shit's all hitting the fan anyway. Might as well tell my story the way it should be told!"

"Can you do it and still keep your identity concealed?" asked Laura, the more practical of the two. "I don't want to get arrested, and I don't think you do either!"

"I think I can do the interview and maintain my anonymity. You'll have to help me, Laura, with that."

"Okay."

Joey then messaged Jerome back and wrote:

Sure, why not. I actually don't live in Queens but I am in the New York City area. Still, for many reasons, it is best if we do the interview over the

Internet so I can maintain my anonymity. I think you understand why.

Within a few minutes, a reply came in from Jerome:

> Okay. I understand why you need to be anonymous. It helps you to be more effective! How about 8:30 tonight? You can put on a mask or have your back to the webcam. Whatever works for you.

"So I guess that's that," said Joey, as he stood up and jumped into his bed with Laura.

"We could do the interview in your living room. I'll run out and buy one of those contraptions that will disguise your voice. The kind kidnappers use. And I can keep your IP address secret...unhackable, and also, we can have you with your face turned away from the webcam."

"Yep. We've set it up for eight thirty."

"We still have some time together before we have to get ready for your interview," said Laura.

"Absolutely. Are you thirsty? I'm going to go get a drink. Would you like a Mountain Mist?"

"You know I don't drink soda. How about some juice or water?" Joey started to smile as he walked out of his bedroom and ran downstairs to get the two of them something to drink.

When he got back, he found Laura on her knees in his bed, bent over, fully naked.

"That's fucking sexy as hell," said Joey, as he put the can of soda and a bottle of water down and jumped onto his bed to join Laura. He began to kiss her whole body, from her chest down to her waist, making her toes curl. She then proceeded to unbutton Joey's pants before ripping off his shirt.

She pushed him down onto his back, where she hopped on top of him, upside-down, performing acts of oral sensation he had never felt before. He then used his tongue to make her wet. The two went at each other for at least an hour like they had a race to win.

"Don't stop, baby," Laura cried every now and then as the two performed oral sex on each other at the same time.

"You like that?" asked Joey.

"Yessss...s"

Several hours later, Joey got a text from a NYC phone number that read:

> We're all set. We're ready to go live. This will be streaming live on the Internet and it will also be archived at my ViewTube channel.

"I think I have to get ready for prime time, Laura," said Joey with excitement and a little fear in his voice.

"Give it all you got, babe," said Laura.

Joey texted back to Jerome:

> I'm ready. Let's get this show on the road.

Jerome texted back:

> No problem

"You sure you want to do this, baby?" asked Laura.

"I'm sure," said Joey.

"All right. I love you, babe," said Laura.

"I love you too, sweetie," Joey said, as he kissed her on the lips.

A few minutes passed, and Jerome was speaking to Joey through his computer, not by texting.

"I'm ready whenever you are."

"Let's do it," replied Joey in a garbled voice completely unrecognizable because of the digitized device.

"I'm going to start recording and when I say 3...2... 1...we will start. Usually I have somebody here with me to do the sound and video, but since we decided to do this interview on such short notice, I couldn't get them out here. So bear with me. I'm gonna try to get through the whole interview by myself. But we should be fine," said Jerome.

"Whenever you're ready, champ," said Joey, as he started to get a little bit nervous. This was his first real media interview, and he wished he had done some media training while awaiting this opportunity, but he would give it his best shot.

Jerome started to shuffle the notecards he had put together that were full of questions as he talked into his webcam.

"So I asked my subscribers what questions I should ask you, and I got some right here, if that is fine with you," said Jerome.

"That's cool man. Whatever works."

"We're going to start in 3...2... 1... and we're live."

Jerome looked over to the video camera as he began.

"Good evening folks, it is Jerome James from Internettica productions. We have a very, very, very special guest tonight. I would like to introduce you all to the man behind the FaceSpace 'God' page. He needs to keep his identity secret, for obvious reasons. But we do know his first name is Joey. We don't know his last name or where he actually lives. Welcome Joey, or should I call you God?""

"Thanks for having me. I'm glad to be on your show, Jerome, and you can call me Joey.

"Now I did ask my Tweeker and ViewTube followers what

questions they had for you, and I got some really good ones. First and foremost, what made you decide to create a page for God on FaceSpace?"

"Actually, Jerome, there was no real reasoning behind it. I made the page years ago when I first heard about FaceSpace. At first, nothing came from it. I maybe got a few hundred likes, but truthfully, I just forgot about the page. I kind of went rogue when it came to social media, you know what I mean?"

"I do," said Jerome. "Did you ever feel wrong when you started to get attention on your God page over the past few months?"

"Not at first. I only started to feel wrong recently, when everything started to dawn on me that what I was doing wasn't so nice. People actually started to believe that I was some sort of higher power or something. It got pretty crazy. But lately, a tragedy happened with one of my friends, and I feel like I am partially to blame."

"What happened to your friend, if you don't mind me asking?"

"I don't want to talk about it too much. Long story short, I gave him a large sum of money, and he used most of it to make a sports bet. He lost. And after he lost it all, he borrowed some more and then lost that. When he couldn't pay back the people he borrowed from, they killed him."

"Wow, that's terrible. And you think you pushed him to start gambling by giving him the money?"

"I knew he once had a gambling problem, but he had been in a support group for it, and he seemed to have the problem licked. I didn't learn his gambling addiction had returned until another friend told me that he was already dead."

"That's tough, man. I'm sorry for your loss."

"Thank you. And the really bad part of it is that I could have easily given him even more money to cover his debt. They didn't have to kill him just because he owed them money!"

"How many people die every day over someone stealing a TV or snatching a purse or even dealing drugs for money?"

"Shit happens, I guess," said Joey.

"But we're getting off topic. So what did you end up doing with the money you raised through your fundmeplease campaign? People were saying you raised over five million dollars. What did you end up doing with all of it?"

"I'm not gonna lie to you bro...at first I spent it recklessly. I had no intention of doing anything good with it. Just wanted to buy myself things. I wanted to get a big house, a car, a bunch of random stuff. Yes, I got a car that cost over $100,000. Even took my boys out and spent like two hundred thousand dollars in one just night with them. I was careless, and it was fucked up."

"So what turned things around?" Jerome asked.

"I wish I could say I independently had an epiphany. But it was definitely my friend's death that jolted me back into reality. That made me see the error of my ways in squandering this gift that I had been given," Joey explained.

"So what happened?" asked the interviewer,

"Well, the other day, I took most of the rest of the money I had, which was still millions, and wrote dozens of checks to different organizations, charities, and foundations, for sick children, starving children, schools, different research organizations for diseases and what not. I contributed everything anonymously, so those organizations are probably receiving those checks right now, as we speak, for $100,000, $500,000, or even $1 million and wondering where it came from. It came from me, but I don't want any credit. Although now I realize I'm a hypocrite since I am talking about it in this interview. But I just want those organizations to keep doing the good work that they're doing. To feed the hungry. To house the homeless. To help those with HIV and AIDS, to find a cure for cancer, heart disease, and autism, to offer arts and physical education for students, to help those with gambling addictions, and to find a cure for Alzheimer's, to name just a few of the charitable causes I donated to."

Joey continued in his disguised voice which sounded like it had cracked a little as he held back his tears.

"I didn't want to feel the pressure of the money anymore. And I just felt wrong having it and using it for frivolous and self-indulgent things. I mean, how many $150 designer shirts can one man wear at a time? So I took some ideas I got from my beloved followers and decided to give most of it away."

"Wow, that's pretty impressive, I must say. So if there's anything you took away from all of this—from having nearly fifty million likes for your "God" page, from getting $5 million in donations, and from your friend's murder, what would it be?"

"That's a very tough question. I certainly got rid of my boredom for a month or two," Joey said, laughing.

There was an awkward moment or two of silence, when Jerome did not respond with laughter to Joey's attempt at a joke.

"But in all seriousness," Joey began, "I'd have to say that power can be a good thing and a bad thing. We as humans too often typically use it in a bad way. But no one man should have too much power, because it changes you. Even with just Internet popularity, my fifteen minutes of fame caused pain in my life. Power makes you realize what type of person you want to be."

"Very deep stuff, Joey. I know you wanted to make this short, so any last words you want to say to the audience?"

"Yeah. Special agent Kenny Owens, you want me so bad. E-mail me privately, and I'll arrange a meeting with you."

"Thank you, whoever you are. This is Jerome James signing off."

"Thanks for believing in me, Jerome," Joey said as the last words of the one and only historic interview that anyone would hear.

Shortly after the interview ended, Joey got a private message at his "God" page. It was from Special Agent Owens, who had been hired by another private security company within a few days of his firing by I.S.I. His new boss agreed that finding out the identity of the creator of the "God" page on FaceSpace was a priority.

"Okay, God-page creator. Let's meet," Special Agent Owens wrote.

Joey wrote back:

Meet me at the shopping mall in Camden, New Jersey, tomorrow night at five o'clock. I'll be in the circle, which is located directly in the middle of the mall. There are carpeted stairs that people wait at. I'll be there. If you want me come get me, I'm not putting up a fight

"That was crazy. Great job, but now what are you going to do?" asked Laura.

"You mean, what are we going to do?"

Joey had shared with Laura the request to meet in person that he had just received from the special agent.

"Are you really going to turn yourself over to that agent?" Laura asked, trying to conceal her fear and confusion.

"I guess so. I don't want this on my conscience anymore. I did something wrong, and I deserve whatever outcome that happens," said Joey, as he hugged Laura then logged onto his FaceSpace page using his cell phone.

He clicked on the 'Write Post' button and began to write:

I am sorry that I have misled you all. I truly didn't mean any harm. I guess when you play with fire you're gonna get burned. My name is Joey Taylor. I grew up and still live in Camden, NJ. I am 26 years old, and I haven't done much in my life. This page is sadly the greatest thing I have accomplished, and I feel I have let you all down. For that I am sorry. I will forever love you all.

Thank you for your support. Thank you for believing in me. If I got anything from this experience that I could give to you, is that we are all God. You, you, and you. Your friend, your mother, brother, sister, father, whoever. You are God. We are all God. God is inside you, in the decisions you make, between right and wrong. Don't follow anything blindly, and always have faith.

This will be my last post. I wish you all good luck. Don't stop believing."

Joey clicked on the button that read 'Publish Post'.

"Done," Joey said.

"What did you do?" asked Laura.

"Just made my final post on the God page."

"Wow, just like that, huh?"

"Yep, just like that. Well, actually, hold up," said Joey before he logged on one more time.

He clicked on the 'Write Post' button and began to type one last time.

Before I sign off for the last time, I have one more request. Everybody please take a second and listen to this upcoming artist, my pal MC Connor.

His new single 'Thank God' is amazing. You can see the video here at www.viewtube.com/MCConnor.

You can also follow him at FaceSpace.com/MCConnor

Much love,
God

Joey clicked 'Publish Post' and then clicked out of the Internet browser.

He then lay down with Laura and tried not to think about the next day when he planned to turn himself in. Laura held him tight and kissed him on the forehead.

Chapter Twenty
The Book of Forgiveness

THE NEXT DAY CAME SOONER than Joey wanted it to. Laura slept over and promised him she wouldn't leave him in this dire time. She woke Joey up with oral sex that morning, and after a couple minutes, he wasn't really in the mood, so he stopped her.

"How about I cook you some eggs or something, baby," he said, as she released him from her mouth.

"I love you, Joey, but I've seen you cook. How about I go cook for us?"

Laura stood up and threw on some of Joey's pajamas and one of his larger t-shirts before heading downstairs to cook for the two of them.

Joey stayed in bed a little while longer, and thought, *Is it really worth turning myself in today? Am I being an idiot?*

He walked downstairs a few minutes later and breathed in the strong scent of bacon. "You really know the way to a man's heart, don't ya?"

"Take a seat. Breakfast will be ready shortly."

The two of them ate bacon, eggs, English muffins with butter melted and jam all over , toasted, with fresh fruit on the side and, of course, Joey's favorite, Mountain Mist.

"This is the best breakfast I've ever had," said Joey.

"You're just saying that."

"Absolutely banging, girl. Just like you. This shit is banging."

The two finished eating, then put their plates in the sink before going back upstairs to have more intimate, passionate sex. It could be the last time Joey would be able to for a long time, if what he thought was going to happen was about to happen. He was expecting to get arrested and then sentenced to at least a year or two in prison. He hadn't consulted a lawyer yet, so he wasn't too sure how much time he was facing, or even what the charges would be but he figured this agent Owens would want to make an example of him. That there are legal consequences for impersonating God through social media? Or was it really a crime? It wasn't like impersonating a doctor or a police officer. But Joey was certain he would probably have to spend some time behind bars because he raised funds under the pretext that he was God even though he donated most of it to good causes and he even set aside enough cash to pay the estimated taxes on his $5 million in donations.

Day turned to night as Joey and Laura got into Joey's sedan and headed downtown to the mall. On the ride there, Joey thought, *Last week I had almost fifty million followers on FaceSpace and five million dollars and next week I could be locked up in the slammer.*

Joey had a call coming in. He answered it and then put it on speaker phone. It was his mother.

"Joseph! I've been looking all over for you. Your second cousin, Jennifer, told me you were on the Internet? She heard about it from Henry, even though you disguised your voice and had your back to the camera. Jennifer said you were interviewed on some website?"

"Yes, Mom. It's not that big of a deal."

"Of course it is. And then what I am also hearing is that you are the one who created that wacky 'God' page on FaceSpace? What is she talking about, Joey?"

"I simply made a page. I didn't think something bad or even anything at all would happen from that page."

"Jennifer was saying something about you might be facing jail time, Joseph?"

"I'm not sure, Mom. I'm going to turn myself in right now."

"What? No, the hell you are. We are going to fight this! Don't turn yourself in. You did nothing wrong."

"I sort of did, Mom. Look, I love you. I am manning up for some mistakes I've made. Tell Dad and Jane, I love them. I love you too. Pray for me. Everything is going to be all right."

"Joey, I'm not kidding. Turn your car around and come home. Let's talk about this."

"No, Mom, I have to go. I'll talk to you later, okay. Just wish me luck."

"Joseph!!"

"Listen, Joey, if people donated money to you like Jennifer said they did because you said you were God, I guess that could be seen in the same light as telling people you're stranded in a strange place and need someone's money to get home. I guess some could consider it a similar kind of fraud, but I don't. You didn't tell those people to believe that you were God. They chose to believe it. It's not the same kind of thing. It's not really fraud."

But Joey had already hung up, and his mother was actually just talking to herself with her parental reasoning that she hoped would exonerate her son from any charges that might get him arrested or jailed.

Joey had already ended the call and, in disgust over the guilt he felt that he might have caused his parents, sister, and Laura, he threw his phone into the center console, as he and Laura pulled into the shopping mall parking lot. Joey found an empty spot and backed in.

Joey started to feel more and more nervous. He put the car in park, turned the key off, and got out of the car. Before Laura could get out, Joey ran around the car to open the passenger door for his girlfriend.

"Thank you, sweetie," said Laura, as she stood outside the car.

"Just want to give a shot to chivalry before I get locked up."

"Shut up. Nothing's going to happen, not if I have anything to say about it."

"No, baby. I am going to take my punishment like a man."

It was almost five o'clock when Joey and Laura entered the front entrance of the mall. They walked down the left wing past the Sneaker Shack and the hair salon.

"I really wish I was back at home, watching Battle Rap videos on ViewTube right about now," said Joey.

"You're going to be fine, Joey," Laura replied.

She drew him closer as they got nearer to the circle in the middle of the mall. As they walked up next to the smoothie stand, Joey saw ten men in black suits all lined up at the bottom of the circle. His nervousness hit an all-time high at that point.

Joey hid behind a wall and pulled Laura with him.

"Holy shit. Those guys look huge and serious. And half of them have guns. I am officially screwed. They're gonna feed me to the wolves."

"Baby, relax," said Laura, as she went in for a big kiss on Joey's sweaty cheek.

"I'm getting nervous, babe."

"I won't let anybody take you. You will be fine."

"Really?"

"Really," said Laura.

Joey grabbed Laura's hand and began to walk. "Okay, let's do this."

They headed down the steps and toward the center of the circle.

Joey walked up to the group of men in suits with his girlfriend on his arm, and said, "Is there an Agent Owens here?"

"Yes, that's me," said Special Agent Kenny Owens, as he

walked out from the group of men. "And you must be Joey Taylor."

"That's me," said Joey.

The group of agents formed a blockade around Joey, Laura, and Agent Owens. Joey became more and more tense as Agent Owens spoke up.

"So you know what you did wrong. We saw your 'oh so humble' interview last night."

"I do, sir. And I am prepared to face the consequences of my actions," said Joey.

"You're making this easier than I thought you would, boy," said the special agent.

"Do what you have to do, Agent Owens."

"Oh I am," said Agent Owens, as he began to roll up his sleeves.

"Let's get this over with," said Joey, as he prepared for the worst.

"I just have to call the local police department, and we will be on our way, Joseph. We'll just wait here until they get here. It won't be much longer. Agent Rogers already made the call when you walked up here."

"I don't understand," said Joey, wondering why Agent Owens was going to drag out the agony of being arrested.

"I work for a private cybersecurity and Internet integrity firm. We don't have the power to actually arrest you, just to pursue offenders, like you, and detain them. Then the local police or federal agents have to come in and do the actual arrest."

"I see. Do your damage," said Joey, as he grasped onto Laura and held her tight.

Joey wondered if the worst part was waiting to be arrested because every one of the minutes that he stood there with Laura, surrounded by Agent Owens and his ten other agents, waiting for the local police or the federal agents to arrive felt like an eternity.

"Let me ask you one thing, son," said Owens. "What in God's name did Billy Brooks, the icon, do to you?"

"Huhh?" said Joey.

"Why the hell did you have to bring Billy Brooks down with you on that awful page of yours?"

"Well, to put it bluntly, he wouldn't take a selfie with us. And I was fucked up on Ecstasy when I hit that motherfucker in the face," said Joey.

Agent Owens' eyes widened and his face turned red.

"You did what?" said the angered Billy Brooks fan.

"Me and my boys fucked up him and his boys. It was epic as fuck."

"You little son of a bitch!" yelled Agent Owens, reflecting on the cancelled Billy Brooks concert that Joey and his antics had caused.

"Whatever, you're a square, dude," said Joey, as Laura kissed him on the cheek and said "Fuck you, you cyber-pig!" and flipped the middle finger to the group of agents.

"Where is the police department? Let's get this kid down to the station already!" yelled Owens.

Just then, a faint rumble came from the right wing of the shopping mall. The noise began to grow louder and louder as a swarm of people came marching toward the circle where Joey and Laura were being detained by agent Owens and his men.

"What is this?" asked Owens.

"I'm not sure, Ken," one of the other agents said.

There had to be a hundred or more people swarming around the circle of Agent Owens, the other agents, Joey, and Laura, filling the stairway as they marched down in front of the agents and Joey.

"You're not taking anybody!" someone shouted.

That man made his way through the crowd, talking into a megaphone.

Joey couldn't believe his eyes.

The man talking through the megaphone was his former

friend Oscar, and beside him was Joey's ex-girlfriend, Amber, as well as his friends Chris and Henry. Joey's sister, Jane, was also there, and so were Joey's mother and father.

The sea of people got closer and closer to Agent Owens, as Oscar stood in front of him and in front of the other agents. In one quick move, Oscar pulled Joey and Laura back away from Agent Owens and the other agents.

"If you want to take Joey, you're going to have to take all of us too! We are his followers!" said Oscar through the megaphone.

From the homemade pretzel place, to the cell phone store, there were people standing close to the circle, standing in support of Joey. They all had been following his God page, and although some were disappointed when they found out the page was created by a mere mortal, and not God, others were very happy with how this anonymous young man had changed his ways and used the money he raised to do good. They had all watched the interview he had on Internettica the night before that streamed live over the Internet.

Two people from the protestors grabbed Laura and pushed her through the crowd, forcing her to blend in with the rest of them. Another two men went over to grab Joey, and they boosted him up in the air, over their shoulders, and crowd-surfed the self-proclaimed 'God' to the back of the sea of protestors, where he essentially faded away into the crowd.

The agents tried to force their way through to get him, but there were too many people holding them back. A few were even shoving some of the agents to the ground. Nobody would let them get to Joey or Laura.

"This isn't the last you will see of us, kid!" yelled Agent Owens, as Joey and Laura disappeared into the determined crowd.

Oscar held his position until the crowd as well as the agents began to back away. The group had been ready and willing to attack the agents, if necessary, but Owens and his accomplices put away their weapons and eventually left the mall.

"You can run, Joey Taylor, but you can't hide," shouted Owens one last time.

Epilogue

A COUPLE OF MONTHS PASSED, and nobody had heard from Joey or Laura in a long time. The 'God' Page had been deactivated right after Joey's final post.

On the bright side, MC Connor reached twenty million views for the new music video he had uploaded on ViewTube called "Thank God."

Record labels all over the country had begun to offer the young rapper countless offers and recording and distribution deals. He turned every offer down at first, claiming, "It wasn't God's plan for him" right now.

But MC Connor soon became the hottest unsigned rapper on

the Internet, selling over ten million copies of his newest mix-tape, via FaceSpace. They said that it was probably due to the mystery business manager that he hired who also had one of the best Internet consultants and social media experts in the business to take care of MC Connor's website, Facespace page, and to make sure his Tweeks and sites were not hacked.

Everyone wanted to know who MC Connor owed his success to, but he wasn't telling.

"All that matters is my music and my message," said MC, as he told the media that he had recently signed his first movie deal for $1 million.

Joey and Laura moved far away to an island thousands of miles from the Tri-State area with some of the money that Joey had put away for savings for the two of them. They planned to start a family in the near future. Joey gave Laura two hundred thousand dollars to start her own app company because she had an idea for an app that they both thought could change the world.

Laura left hacking behind in her past life. The mobile application was called Decorat3D. And it combined home decoration and 3D printing. She already had a few potential investors interested, with MC Connor as one of them.

Joey decided social networking wasn't all that bad. So he

updated his personal FaceSpace page and added many friends and family from his past.

He decided to change his profile picture to a photo of him and Laura posing together in front of the ocean, outside their cute, little island home.

He proceeded to click on the 'Write Post' button and typed:

> How is everybody?! Sorry I've been gone for a long time, but I had a religious breakthrough as of late. I guess you can say I've been "born again" LOLOL. Anyways, glad to be back. Thanking God every day to be alive #Amen."

Joey clicked '*Publish Post*' before he reached down to take a sip from an older can of Mountain Mist.

He suddenly spit out the liquid all over his laptop screen, realizing he had just gulped piss.

The End

About the Authors

Jeff Yager grew up in Stamford, Connecticut; he now resides in a suburb of Tampa, Florida. A rapper and a wrestler, Jeff is also the author of the sci-fi novel, *Atom and Eve* (www.atomandeve-thenovel.com).

Skye Bynes grew up in Norwalk, Connecticut. After several years in Alabama, he now lives in a suburb of Tampa, Florida where he works for a major food service company. *I Like God* is his first novel.

In addition to co-authoring *I Like God* together, Jeff Yager and Skye Bynes are friends.